POISONED
Primrose

DAHLIA DONOVAN

TANGLED TREE PUBLISHING

POISONED PRIMROSE

MOTTS COLD CASE MYSTERY BOOK 1

DAHLIA DONOVAN

The Grasmere Cottage Mystery Trilogy

Dead in the Garden - Dead in the Pond - Dead in the Shop

Motts Cold Case Mystery Series

Poisoned Primrose

Stand-alone Romances

After the Scrum

At War With A Broken Heart

Forged in Flood

Found You

One Last Heist

Pure Dumb Luck

Here Comes The Son

All Lathered Up

Not Even A Mouse

The Misguided Confession

The Sin Bin Series

The Wanderer - The Caretaker - The Royal Marine -

The Botanist - The Unexpected Santa

The Lion Tamer - Haka Ever After

Poisoned Primrose © 2020 by Dahlia Donovan

All rights reserved. No part of this book may be used or reproduced in any written, electronic, recorded, or photocopied format without the express permission from the author or publisher as allowed under the terms and conditions with which it was purchased or as strictly permitted by applicable copyright law. Any unauthorized distribution, circulation or use of this text may be a direct infringement of the author's rights, and those responsible may be liable in law accordingly. Thank you for respecting the work of this author.

Poisoned Primrose is a work of fiction. All names, characters, events and places found therein are either from the author's imagination or used fictitiously. Any similarity to persons alive or dead, actual events, locations, or organizations is entirely coincidental and not intended by the author.

For information, contact the publisher, Tangled Tree Publishing.

www.tangledtreepublishing.com

Editing: Hot Tree Editing

Cover Designer: BooksSmith Design

E-book ISBN: 978-1-922359-18-6

Paperback ISBN: 978-1-922359-19-3

For Meg, Renee, Debbie, and Jennifer, who help turn my first drafts into something magical.

CHAPTER ONE

A cat, a turtle, and a Pineapple walk into a cottage.... That's it. That's the punch line of my life choices.

"Well, here we are." Motts closed the solid wooden front door to her new cottage, leaning back against it and releasing a pent-up sigh. She opened her bluish-grey eyes to stare at all the boxes, plastic bins, and bags. "Bugger. You've no one to blame but yourself for this, Pineapple Mottley."

Pineapple Meg Mottley had been so named because her mother had craved nothing but the tropical fruit during her one and only pregnancy. There'd only been one issue. No one ever called her Pineapple; her uncle had nicknamed her Motts as an infant, and it stuck.

Meow.

The plaintive cry came from behind one of the boxes. Motts moved quickly to lift up her precious cat. Cactus was a tortoiseshell Sphynx cat; she'd found the poor dear at a shelter and fallen head-over-sneakers in love. He buried his head in her shoulder-length brown hair, purring his little heart out.

She stroked the suede-like downy fuzz covering his wrinkly body. "What are we going to do about this mess? Want to help me unpack? No?"

Figures.

What have I gotten myself into?

When her auntie Daisy had passed away, Motts had taken the inherited cottage as a sign. London had always been overwhelming to her senses. Polperro was a much quieter place with a slower pace suited for her autistic needs.

She loved Polperro. Her parents were both originally from Cornwall. A lot of her family lived in the area, as did her ex-girlfriend.

Despite having spent many a holiday with family at the cottage, Motts found herself overwhelmed by the sudden change. *This was a terrible idea. I should've sold the house. I am such a silly fool.*

Okay.

Take a few deep breaths.
Match Cactus's purring.
You're going to be okay.

"Ahh!" She jumped when a rapid knocking on the door jolted her. "For goodness sake."

"Motts? You okay?"

She spun around and yanked the door open to find the welcome sight of her ex-girlfriend, Pravina Griffin, and Vina's twin brother, Nish. "I'm...."

How do I finish the sentence?
Panicked?
In the middle of the biggest mistake I've ever made?
Just slightly overcome by irrational fear?

Nish moved forward to take Cactus from her arms while Vina led her inside. "Amma is bringing over supper. She wanted to let the sambar simmer a little longer. She even made your favourite kind of rice."

The Griffin twins took after their Tamil mother, Leena, who'd been a Bollywood star before falling in love with Cadan Griffin, a Cornish-Indian cricket player. They'd settled in Polperro to run a coffee shop and bakery. Griffin Brews had been around for thirty-plus years, and now their children managed it, allowing their parents to retire early.

Leena and Cadan had welcomed Motts with open

arms even before she'd briefly dated their daughter. Motts and Vina had realised over the years that their close bond felt more like that of siblings. They'd dumped each other but remained the best of friends, where they'd started in the first place.

"Let's talk about something less daunting than unpacking. How goes the dating life? Did you fill out a dating profile on the site I emailed you?" Vina plucked Moss, Motts's turtle, out of his travel terrarium. "Well?"

"No, I didn't. There's no box to check for asexual, biromantic autistic." Motts gently took Moss to return her to a safer place. "No touching the turtle."

"I won't drop Moss." Vina thankfully turned her attention to the nearest box. "This says 'bedroom' on it."

"Congrats on being able to read." Nish poked his sister in the side. "Why don't we start with the kitchen? Motts can direct so we don't mess with her space. We can ignore the bags of patterned paper."

Bags of paper lined one entire side of the living room. Motts made and sold origami floral arrangements for people who loved flowers but suffered from allergies. She'd made a decent living with her Hollyhock Folded Blooms business, and working from home was an added bonus.

"Me? Make a mess?" Vina feigned great offence.

"Mess is basically your middle name." Nish knew his sister well. He turned dark brown eyes towards Motts. "Well, fruity one? Are you ready to make sense of chaos?"

"Nope. Probably why I dumped her." Motts grinned so Vina would know it was a joke. She was never wholly sure people would understand her sense of humour. "What am I doing?"

"Showing independence?"

"I'm thirty-nine. A bit late to become an adult." She'd lived with her parents in London even while attending university. This would be her first attempt at being alone in a home. "I'm having hot flashes. Is it too late to learn how to be a grown-up?"

"It's never too late. Look at Nish. He's still waiting on a growth spurt," Vina teased her twin brother. They were only two years younger than Motts. "Well? Where do you want to start?"

Motts glanced between the twins and the stacks of her belongings. "The mug box. We'll want tea to get us through the evening."

They needed coffee, not tea. Motts's kettle and blue-patterned mugs were unpacked first. Then, they methodically made their way through every box with "kitchen" on it.

After a warm and filling supper of pumpkin sambar (delicious tamarind spiced stew) and fragrant steamed rice, Motts and the Griffin clan made short work of the boxes. Nish and his father carried bedroom items upstairs but left them for her to go through. Some things she had to do for herself.

Once the Griffins had gone, Motts made sure Moss was settled in their new home, grabbed her mug of hot chocolate, and clambered up the stairs with Cactus close behind. She sat on the edge of her bed, close to tears.

What am I feeling?

Fear.

Maybe.

Am I overwhelmed?

Probably.

Taking a few deep breaths, Motts reminded herself that moving into the cottage was the right decision. Her aunt had left the two-story home on the cliff overlooking the Polperro harbour to her only niece. If Auntie Daisy could live alone, Motts thought she'd manage on her own just fine.

Hopefully.

The following morning, Motts woke to find Cactus curled up under the blanket beside her. He tended to be more of a burrower than the average kitty.

She left him snoozing to find coffee and get the fire going.

Sunlight was already filtering in through the windows. Motts managed to avoid bashing her knee against the various boxes in her path. February had been an unusually cold month, and a warm fire would defrost her frozen toes.

First, she went through her morning routine. *Clean teeth, clean face, get dressed.* Her whole day would get thrown out of whack if she didn't follow her usual schedule as best as possible.

If hot flashes were at all useful, they'd heat my feet.

"I have made fire!" Motts exclaimed. She waited for a few minutes to make sure the whole cottage wasn't about to go up in flames. "Success."

Coffee and a plate of Jaffa Cakes made the best breakfast to wake her up. *I'm an adult. I can eat biscuits for breakfast. Perfectly legitimate. And Mum's not here to lecture me about my teeth falling out.*

Grabbing a second mug of coffee, she wandered over to stare out the back window at the garden. She hoped there was a garden underneath the overgrown mess. Her auntie had definitely allowed her flowers, weeds, and other greenery to run wild when she'd gotten sick.

Motts pinched the bridge of her nose to stop a

sneeze. "Don't be dramatic. You can't smell the pollen from inside the cottage. It's not even warm enough for the flowers to be blooming yet."

Allergies had always been a plague for Motts. She loved gardening, but flowers were her nemesis. *I suppose I can have Auntie Daisy's caretaker come out to clean things up for me.*

Is that lazy?

It's lazy.

Meow.

"Morning. The sun is up. Do you want to watch me work in the garden?" Motts lifted her beloved cat up. She set him on the bench by the large picture window. "I've already put your breakfast out."

With Cactus's high metabolism, Motts made sure he had sufficient meals and snacks throughout the day. She gave him a quick snuggle. He purred his contentment against her cheek.

"What do you think is going to give first? My allergies or my energy?" She gently set him down on his mound of blankets. They'd been one of the first things she'd unpacked. "Well, the weeds won't pull themselves, will they?"

Some days, Motts enjoyed taking Cactus outside with her, but his sensitive skin made it impossible in the cold and windy February morning. She didn't even want to be out there.

But she needed to trim back the chaos of the garden. It had bothered her all night. She'd had nightmares of weeds and vines taking over the house, strangling her to death.

No.

The garden had to be cleared out completely. Her mind wouldn't settle otherwise. She knew herself well enough. And she had to do it.

Grabbing gloves and garden tools from the box by the back door, Motts made her way out into the bright sunshine. She paused to listen to the glorious sound of wind and waves. Polperro had always been one of her favourite places in the world; she'd never understood how her parents had moved away.

Cornwall had to be the most magnificent place in the world. Both sides of her family had lived along the sea, going back generations. It was no wonder she felt most at home here.

"What are you doing?"

Motts dropped her spade and fell backwards into a pile of weeds. "What?"

"What the hell do you think you're doing?" a handsome young man she'd never seen shouted over the gate at her. "Who said you could muck about in the garden?"

"It's my garden." Motts mustered her courage to get to her feet, holding the spade tightly in her hands. "My cottage. My garden. Naff off."

"You're the fruit girl."

"Pineapple." She refused to back down while glaring at his nose. "Who are you?"

"Danny Orchard. I used to help my granddad and dad care for the garden." He sounded calmer, but she kept a hold of her makeshift weapon. "Sorry if I scared you."

"I'm cleaning out the weeds." Motts ignored the hand he was holding out across the gate. "Have a nice morning."

"Right."

Motts returned to the weeds and didn't look up until she heard his footsteps heading away. "*Fruit* girl. What a berk."

After the strange encounter, Motts withdrew quickly into the cottage. She wanted stone walls between her and the outside world. At times, the best method of self-care was to retreat into a safe space.

Weeds could wait. They weren't going to crawl away. She had to bleed off all the weird energy leftover from being shouted at.

Confrontation never came easily to her. Motts tended to shut down and lose her ability to formulate a coherent response. She barely managed to muddle through.

She wrapped up in a heavy blanket in front of the fire with Cactus curled up in her lap. "Next time, we'll stay in bed."

Meow.

CHAPTER TWO

Lemon curd on buttered toast soothed a multitude of problems. Motts had made three slices to get her through the morning. She hadn't quite recovered despite spending an entire day alone in the cottage.

Although needing more time to recover, Motts had several early meetings. Vina had helped her connect with a few shop owners in Polperro. She hoped to convince them to consider commissioning some of her paper flower arrangements.

Motts stared mournfully into her empty mug. "Can I take a sick day?"

Meow.

She ran her fingers gently over Cactus's head,

rubbing behind his ears. "Is that a yes or a no? Or do you not want to be left behind?"

I could have another piece of toast.

Procrastinating won't erase your need to meet Marnie and Peggie.

It helped Motts that she knew both women. She'd met them several times on the Mottley family holidays to Polperro. They were lovely people who'd make her feel welcome and comfortable.

And yet, her anxiety refused to settle.

She had a lifetime of experience forcing herself to get through dealing with the world. Her autistic diagnosis had come late—in her midthirties. She'd felt relief at having answers, yet in some ways, even four years on, she continued to struggle to adjust to the paradigm shift.

Changing out of her comfy pyjamas into jeans and a long-sleeved flannel shirt, Motts stood in front of the full-length mirror on the back of the bedroom door. *You can do this. Origami flowers are your bread and butter. Talk about the paper arrangements—you don't need to make small talk.*

Motts redid the buttons on her shirt. "I'm Motts."

You don't have to introduce yourself. You've met them before. They know your name.

"Right." She didn't make eye contact with her reflection. "Okay. Hello. Lovely to see you again."

Do I ever say lovely to see you?

No.

"Hi. Do you want to buy my flowers?" *Great. Now I sound like some Victorian street urchin without the accent and coal-smudged face.* "Hello. Thanks for meeting with me. I brought sketches."

Well, it's better. Not brilliant, but better.

She pulled on an oversized grey hoodie that had originally belonged to her younger and much taller cousin, River. She'd stolen it from him last year. He hadn't complained—much.

"You can do this." Motts tried to summon the courage to leave for her first appointment. She refused to be late. "If we're doing this, we're going now."

With an apologetic pet to Cactus and Moss for leaving them behind, Motts raced out the door. She shivered in the brisk breeze off the sea. *Hello, February in Cornwall. I'll just be here freezing my toes off.*

Grabbing her blue bicycle, Motts secured her sketchbook in the left pannier bag and her backpack in the right one. Her bike was her pride and joy. A 3-speed Pure City Step-Through in seafoam green with dusty pink vegan leather seat and handles. She'd had it customised with the saddlebags and a wire basket in the front. Her dad had paid for it to be shipped over from the maker in Los Angeles.

She adored it. And not just because it matched her seafoam green Vespa scooter. She thought both modes of transportation would be perfect for living in a tiny village.

Pausing to glance behind her, she once again found herself appreciating the beauty of the area. Her auntie had inherited the cottage many years ago from her great-uncle. Their family had a long history in Cornwall.

Motts could understand why they'd clung on to the cottage; it was ideally situated up almost at the top of a hill above Polperro. She had a stunning view of the coastline and across the village itself. In the bright early spring morning, the harbour practically sparkled like someone had dumped glitter into the sea.

After carefully making her way down the narrow stone stairs, Motts hopped on her bicycle. She pedalled her way to Marnie Shaw's Bridal Lace Designs for the first meeting. Her nerves kicked into high gear—and her fingers refused to work the buckles on the saddlebag.

Bugger.

"Want a hand?"

Motts glanced up to find her cousin River Chen-

Mottley standing across the street next to his car. "I have two hands."

River crossed the street and waited for her to move her fingers out of the way. "Vina sent me a text earlier. She thought you might want some moral support."

"Could've brought Cactus."

"Cactus can't speak and doesn't have a degree in business." River made short work of undoing the buckles. "Ready for the big presentation?"

She took her sketchbook and bag from him. "Mostly."

"You'll be fine, Motts." He reached out to straighten her jacket. "You can always imagine them naked."

"Why on earth would I do that?" Motts frowned at him in confusion.

"It helps you feel less afraid."

"How?" She thought it would make things worse, if anything. "Nudity tends to amp up the awkward to a maximum."

"Only a suggestion." River nodded towards the bridal shop. "Are we going in? Or do you want a minute to gather your thoughts?"

"Don't let me embarrass myself," she muttered.

"I have complete confidence in your ability. I'm only here to do the heavy lifting. Carry your sketchbook. Think of me as a prop holder." River opened the book to one of the drawings. "See?"

"Come on." Motts knew her cousin had enough of the Mottley stubbornness not to back down. He also shared her slightly off-kilter sense of humour. "I can't rehearse this in my head anymore. I'll forget something. Did you cut your hair?"

"Mum threatened to take a trimmer to my head if I didn't." He tilted his head and gave her a wide smile. "What do you think?"

"The left side is slightly longer than the right."

"Well, that's filled me with confidence." River snickered. He pulled the door and held it for her. "You're a terrible wingman."

"I'm not a man—and I sadly lack wings." She flapped her arms. "No lift."

They laughed together, though Motts wasn't entirely confident she understood why.

Her first presentation went well. Marnie loved her floral arrangements—perfect during the winter season and for any bride worried about allergies. They put together a loose plan for commission work along with a few standard pieces that could sit in the shop.

Her luck ran out at the second meeting of the day with Peggy Shine, who ran a local shop that catered to tourists. Motts stumbled over her words. She forgot everything she'd practised in front of the mirror.

In her panic and embarrassment, Motts ran out of the shop, bumping into the doorframe in the process. She rubbed her arm while standing outside in the cool air. *Why? Why? Why do I do this to myself every time?*

Wanting to put space between herself and her humiliation, Motts got on her bike to pedal away as quickly as she could. She strained to get her bicycle up one of the steep hills leading up to the cliffs, eventually pulling over to the side and sitting on a nearby railing.

When her breathing finally returned to normal, Motts glanced around in surprise. She'd made it further out of Polperro than she'd realised. *Bugger.* River would be worried; she'd abandoned her meeting and her things with her poor cousin.

When she'd been a young woman, her family had made excuses for her behaviour. "Don't mind Motts, she suffers from poor nerves." Anxiety might've been one problem, but being autistic had answered more questions than having a "nervous disposition" ever had.

Knowing why she had meltdowns over stressful situations helped—it didn't make the problems go away. Motts wrapped her arms around herself. She wanted to be home with her cat and turtle, not sitting on a guardrail along the road; it would take her a good twenty minutes to cycle back.

"Miss Mottley?"

Motts lifted her head up to find a police car had pulled up beside her. She'd gotten so lost in her thoughts, she hadn't heard. "Sorry?"

"Constable Hugh Stone." He stepped out of his vehicle and came over to her. "Are you alright? Inspector Ash's wife gave him a call. She said you'd had a panic attack. The inspector wanted me to see if you wanted a ride back home."

"I can manage."

"Sure. But the wind's blowing something fierce. We wouldn't want to fly off the cliff or tumble down the road, would we? Marnie's a harsher taskmaster than the inspector." Constable Stone kept his voice low and glanced over his shoulder dramatically. "Think she can hear me?"

"Not from the village." Motts had to smile when she realised he was trying to help her relax. "I'd appreciate a lift, Constable. Thank you."

"Hughie. Everyone calls me Hughie." He gave her a broad grin. "And welcome to Polperro. Heard you moved into the cottage up on the hill. You let me know if you run into any trouble."

"In Polperro?" She'd always found the place so safe and calm.

"My job's to keep everyone safe." He carefully secured her bicycle on the bike rack at the back of his car. "Hop in. We'll get you home in the warmth in no time. And I'll give River a call to meet us there."

Great.

I'll be dealing with an overconcerned cousin and a curiously cautious constable.

Crikey.

Slow down.

And where did crikey come from?

Okay, that might've been one too many c-words.

"Everything okay?" He paused by the door when she started to laugh.

Motts waved him off. "Sorry. Made myself laugh."

"Right."

Brilliant.

The constable chatted cheerfully all the way to her cottage. He carried her bike up the steps and helped secure it by the side of the house. Motts invited him in, but he left once River arrived a few minutes later.

River followed her into the cottage. He set her sketchbook and bag on the table by the door. "Want me to whip up some hot chocolate? We can have toast, drink away our sorrows, and gossip about the family."

"Gossip?" Motts narrowed her eyes while River took over her kitchen. He made better hot chocolate than she did. No matter how many times her dad tried to show her how to make the family recipe. "What's happened now?"

"Why don't you feed your menagerie while I get the hot chocolate going?" River nudged her towards Moss. "I'll tell you all about my dad getting lost and almost driving off a mountain."

"I'm sorry, what did you just say?" Motts froze in the process of cutting up a bit of apple for her turtle to snack on. "How do you almost drive off a mountain?"

"Well, you get lost. In the dark. You go too fast around a corner, drive off the road, past the guardrail, and down the embankment." River stirred the pot of cream on the hob gently. "A tree stopped them, so technically they didn't go all the way off the mountain."

"Goodness." Motts rested her hand on her chest. "Are they hurt?"

"Pretty sure dad's pride hasn't recovered. Mum keeps prodding him about his driving." He broke off a couple pieces of chocolate to prepare to throw into the pot. "They're fine."

"They drove off a mountain."

"Pretty much."

"Off a mountain," Motts repeated the words a few more times. "I'm never riding with your parents ever again."

"Wise decision."

Over their impromptu late lunch or early tea, River updated her on all the family gossip. He also handed over an order from Peggy. She'd been sold on all the designs despite Motts having a meltdown and running out of the shop.

Not her best moment.

"Are your parents coming down from London?" River gathered up their plates and set the dishes in the sink for her. He knew her well enough to know she preferred doing the cleaning up herself. "You know my mum and dad would be here in a heartbeat if you asked."

Uncle Tom, or Uncle Tomato, as she called him, was her dad's brother. They lived in Looe, next door to her grandparents. Her extended family tended to be less smothering than her parents.

Her mum and dad struggled to see her as a grown adult. They'd always been supportive. But even before her official diagnosis, they'd often been *overly* helpful.

Her auntie, uncle, cousin, and grandparents, on the other hand, all encouraged her to simply do her best. If she wanted help, they'd be there. She appreciated their being willing to let her struggle along without interfering.

"Motts?"

She glanced up from her hot chocolate. "Sorry?"

"Are your parents coming to visit?"

"They're letting me be independent." Motts hadn't understood the edge in her mum's voice at the time.

"You're thirty-nine years old."

"I'm aware." She didn't know if her parents understood. "Maybe they need time to adjust to my moving out here by myself."

"Even if you're almost forty and completely capable of managing your life?" River stretched his arm across the little kitchen table to squeeze her hand. "They'll come around."

"Mum probably thinks I'll come home sobbing like a child."

"You'll prove her wrong." He sounded so confident.

"I ran out of the shop." Motts covered her face with her hand, feeling embarrassed.

"And? You had a brilliant first meeting. And next time, you'll know to only plan one meeting per day—or maybe a week." River squeezed her other hand gently. "Just because it takes you longer, doesn't make you any less of an amazingly talented human being."

CHAPTER THREE

Two days after the meeting debacle, Motts emerged from hibernating in her cottage. She'd spent her time making flowers and a list of changes to make in the garden.

On top of the list? Digging up and clearing out the flower beds, removing the stone pile in the corner, and preparing the ground for a herb garden. Motts's allergies prevented her from growing anything floral.

Her call to her auntie's old gardener had been odd. Mr Orchard had said no. A firm negative. He'd ranted and raved at her for almost a full two minutes. And then he'd hung up on her.

The conversation hadn't gone any better than the one with his grandson. Yet, Motts couldn't help wondering if she'd offended them without knowing. What was she supposed to do about the garden?

After a lengthy text thread with Nish, Vina, and River, Motts had sent an email to the friendly constable who'd brought her home. Apparently, during the low tourist season, Hughie helped out around the village. He'd responded quickly, promising to come over the following morning to start work.

And he had.

"I'll get these stones moved. Do you want to save them? If not, I can repurpose them in another garden so they're not wasted." Hughie hefted several into his wheelbarrow. "Are you sure I can't help with anything other than this section? I don't mind pulling weeds."

"Okay." Motts shrugged. She wanted to say no—but saying no was hard. "Okay."

It took an hour to clear out the sectioned-off plot in the garden. Hughie moved on to the pile of stones while Motts began preparing the ground for her herb garden. She planned to use them to make a border for the various vegetables that would go in at a later date.

It would be better than working in an allotment like she'd done in London. People had an unnecessary need to chat while gardening. She wanted to be left alone.

Then again, Motts wanted to be left alone most days.

"Is your phone handy?"

Motts sat back on her heels. She'd been digging in the dirt while Hughie went back and forth with the stones in his wheelbarrow to the four-yard skip she'd rented at his suggestion. He'd gotten down to the last bit. "Define handy?"

"Mine's in my car—staying dry and clean." Hughie had turned more serious than she'd seen him. He tugged off his gloves, tossing them into the wheelbarrow. "Do you have a mobile phone?"

Motts stared at him, trying to process his urgency before finally shaking her head and reaching down for her phone. "Here. What's happened?"

"I'd like you to go inside the house. Get warm, have some tea, and stay there." Hughie wasted no time making his phone call. "Go on."

Walking towards the house, Motts glanced back over her shoulder when she heard him mention finding a hand. *Did he say fingers? Actual fingers? What the devil is going on? Was there a person under the pile of stones? Can't be. Too absurd to be true.*

Motts did make tea. She did get the fire going. But she *didn't* ignore the drama playing out in her garden. "What do you think he found, Cactus?"

Her cat stretched out before hopping into her lap. Motts had curled up in the comfortable recliner set up by the window. Her aunt had loved gazing out into the garden and had spent many hours in the chair.

Hughie tapped on the window and pointed to the door. "Can I come in?"

"Go on." Motts nodded.

He wiped his feet on the mat outside and then came into the cottage. "Oh, it's lovely and warm in here."

She took her phone when he handed it over. "What's happening?"

Hughie crouched by the fire, holding his hands out to warm them. "I'm not sure how to put this delicately."

"I'm not a wilting rose. Don't be delicate." She cuddled Cactus to her chest. *Cuddly, curious, creature. Stop it, Motts, pay attention.* "You found something."

He rubbed his hands together while staring into the flames. It was almost a full minute before he turned to face her. "I can't give you all the details. I'm only a constable. I'm sure Inspector Ash will be by later to speak with you. You're going to have to put off any further changes in your garden."

"Why?"

"I found a body underneath the pile of stones. I

think. There are definitely skeletal remains." Hughie stood back up. "I'll wait outside for the coroner. Inspector Ash should be along soon. Please stay inside, alright?"

"Alright."

It wouldn't keep her from keeping an eye on the happenings through the window. Criminal investigations had always been an obsession of hers. This body wasn't the first she'd found.

As a young girl, Motts had had the misfortune of finding the lifeless body of her only school friend. She'd been walking through a park on her way home from school when a splash of colour underneath a hedge caught her attention. Jenny's coat. They'd never found the killer.

And Motts had never forgotten. She'd become fixated on cold cases, watching documentaries, reading articles and books on the subject. Her parents had eventually intervened, so she'd hidden her interest.

Even now, all these years later, Motts periodically checked to see if Jenny's case had been solved. It hadn't. She knew it likely never would be.

And unanswered questions tended to worry at Motts continually.

"Why in the world is a body buried in Auntie

Daisy's garden?" Motts had a feeling the police would have the same question. "What if they think I did it?"

Cactus offered a meow of comfort, then butted his head against her hand. She patted him absently, her attention focused entirely on the activity in her garden.

Caution tape had gone up around the corner where the stones had been. Hughie had talked with a tall man who Motts thought might be Marnie's husband—the local inspector. She knew some of the police force was split between several local villages, given how tiny they were.

She moved away from her perch by the window to feed Moss a snack, give Cactus one of his many meals, and cobble something together for lunch. "What do you think happened?"

Her cat, as always, didn't answer. He did purr at her. She swore he understood her every word—pity she couldn't return the favour.

"Ms Mottley?"

Motts glanced over to find the inspector standing in the door. "Yes?"

"Do you mind answering a few questions?" He showed her his ID. "I'm Inspector Ash."

"No. I mean, yes. Or, no. I'm going to stop now."

Motts grabbed her toast when it popped up. "Hungry?"

His lips twitched at the corners. "Thank you, no. You've just moved in, am I right? Have you seen anyone in your garden?"

"Aside from Cactus?"

"Cactus."

Motts pointed to her cat. "Cactus."

He turned his head to the side to cough a few times. "Aside from your cat."

"Not really. Given the state of it, not sure anyone spent time in the garden after Auntie Daisy fell ill. Not even her gardener." Motts provided him with information on the Orchards—including her mild confrontation with the youngest member of the family. "Is it a body, then?"

"I'll let you know when we've wrapped things up out there. It might take a while, though." He closed his notebook and slipped it into his pocket. "Hugh passed me your number, so I'll give you a ring if I have any further questions."

Motts watched him leave, then glanced over at Cactus. "He said yes without saying yes."

With a live-action drama developing in front of her, Motts spent the rest of the day sitting by the window. The police eventually left when night fell.

Inspector Ash had left a constable to watch over the crime scene, as the techs hadn't quite finished.

They apparently intended to check every inch of the garden for evidence. Motts guessed they were concerned additional victims might be found. She felt as though her quiet little cottage had been violated.

Motts dragged her blanket more tightly around her and Cactus. *Did Auntie Daisy know a body was buried in her garden? She couldn't have, right? How in the world did that poor soul wind up under the stones? And when?*

"Knock, knock."

Motts was so startled by the sudden voice outside her window that she knocked Cactus to the floor. "Sorry, love."

Remembering how to breathe, Motts glanced over to find the Griffin twins grinning at her. They waved cheerfully. She wondered if the constable outside the cottage would consider chasing them away.

Probably not.

"You are *not* funny," Motts grumbled after retrieving Cactus from the floor and letting the twins inside.

"Sorry." Nish's apology sounded a lot more sincere than Vina's. "Are you doing alright?"

"Fine." Motts retreated to her cosy chair with

Cactus shifting around to get comfortable in her lap once again. "You're out late."

"Amma heard from Hughie when he stopped into the coffee shop that the police had cordoned off your garden." Vina dropped onto the sofa with a groan, stretching out and forcing her brother to sit on the arm. "Did they really find a body?"

"*Pravina.*" Nish shoved her foot when she playfully pushed him off the couch. "You can't pepper her with questions before we've bribed her with food. Honestly. Have you never heard of subtlety?"

"Subtlety goes over Motts's head." Vina reached down to lift up the bag they'd brought. "Amma made chicken chettinad and roti. We grabbed Jaffa Cakes for dessert."

"Food?" Motts latched on to the relevant part of the sibling bickering. Chicken curry and flatbread sounded terrific. "I have no problem talking for my supper."

CHAPTER FOUR

"Bugger." Motts tossed her third attempt at a calla lily into the rubbish bin. "Will you focus?"

She hadn't slept well, knowing a constable stood sentry. Well, he sat in his car outside her cottage. He'd appreciated the mug of tea and heated-up leftovers she'd taken out to him for breakfast.

After her own breakfast, Motts had sat down by the coffee table to fold paper. She had Etsy orders along with samples for both the bridal shop and gift shop to fulfil. Focusing had definitely not been easy.

The forensic team had returned around ten in the morning. They'd made the drive from Plymouth, since Polperro was too small a village to have a dedicated CSI force. She was honestly surprised they had an inspector.

Inspector Ash had been a closed book when he stopped in to say hello. Motts hadn't been courageous enough to pepper him with questions. She'd wanted to, though.

Thankfully, the internet didn't require small talk or conversation. A quick search pulled up multiple forum posts regarding missing persons within the region. Motts focused on the ones in and around Polperro.

She found three.

Which one of these are you?

One of the names did stand out to her. Rhona Walters, a local woman, who ran The Salty Seaman—a fish and chip shop started by her father, who'd been a merchant marine. She and her older brother Innis had inherited the popular business. Motts found a number of articles about her disappearance several years ago.

How had no one realised she'd been buried in a shallow grave under stones in Auntie Daisy's garden? How had no one smelled the body? The Orchards regularly had, up until the last six months of her aunt's life, kept up with the yard. How did they not notice?

A comment under the first article when she'd disappeared caught Motts attention. The wording sounded extremely emotional. The commenter had railed against the local police for not doing enough, accusing them of conspiracy. Were they protesting too much? Was this a family member or lover who'd grown desperate?

How long does it take for a body to completely decompose?

Hughie had specifically mentioned skeletal remains. Rhona had been missing for close to two years. Was that sufficient time given where she'd been buried?

She wondered if the police had found any jewellery. Clothes might not survive, but metal surely would. One of the articles had explicitly mentioned a necklace Rhona had always worn.

Meow.

Cactus hopped up on the coffee table. He launched himself at one of the violets she'd made. The mischievous feline slid across the slick surface and narrowly missed her mug of tea.

He sat on his haunches and gave her a look of pure kitty aggravation. *Hiss.*

"Don't act as though I betrayed you. No one asked you to audition for skating on ice." Motts lifted her grumbling cat into her arms. "Are you hungry? Have I neglected your many, many needs?"

After dropping a snack into Moss's terrarium, Motts silenced Cactus's complaining with one of his favourite treats—baked tuna croutons with a hint of catnip. Her precious Sphynx practically inhaled the little biscuits. She'd caught him trying to get into the jar several times. Tricky beast.

Motts left him to rolling around on the carpet in front of the fire with his crouton. She gathered up all the intricately folded violets; they'd been made with a specially chosen paper for one of her Etsy customers. The order had to be shipped by the end of the week.

A knock on her back door pulled her away from carefully packing the violets into a box. Motts found Inspector Ash with a large man wearing a slightly wrinkled suit. He stood a good bit taller than everyone in the garden—the giant teddy bear of Hughie included.

"Hello." Motts shoved her hands into the pockets of her cardigan. She tried not to stare at the intimidating mountain of a man. Her eyes stayed on the crooked pin on his tie. "Did you identify the body?"

"I—" Inspector Ash started.

"We're not releasing any information." Officer Intimidation cut him off sharply. Inspector Ash didn't seem happy with his new friend. "I'm Detective Inspector Teo Herceg with the Plymouth Cold Case Unit."

Motts glanced between the two men without

meeting either of their eyes. "Does Plymouth often send officers out to Polperro?"

"The chief inspector decided we could use the expertise of DI Herceg, given the state of the victim." Inspector Ash seemed to disagree with his boss. "We had a few more questions."

"Oh?" Motts eyed them before stepping to the side to invite them into the cottage. She didn't want to risk Cactus trying to sneak outside. "How can I help?"

The detectives settled together on the couch while Motts made tea. She offered them bourbon biscuits—no one got her Jaffa Cakes. No one. Not even scary police officers who wouldn't stop staring at her turtle.

A series of questions followed about her auntie, her family, the cottage, and her connections to Polperro. The rapid-fire intensity made her mind spin. She struggled to comprehend each question, never mind answer.

The shutdown hit before Motts had time to withdraw herself from the conversation. Her mind went black, as though someone had hit the off switch on her ability to formulate complete sentences. *Yes. No. Maybe. Yes. No. Maybe.* She couldn't even ask them to leave.

"Ms Mottley? Can you answer the question,

please?" Inspector Ash repeated himself several times. "Ms Mottley? Are you feeling okay?"

She shook her head, then nodded. Cactus leapt up into her lap. He sat and faced the two detectives.

Inspector Herceg held up his hand to stop Ash from pushing her. He leaned forward on the couch. "My cousin is autistic. She gets tangled in her head and sometimes needs space to find her way out. I apologise if I'm making assumptions. But I'm even sorrier if we've caused you distress."

Motts rocked slightly in her comfy chair. "Okay."

He pulled a card out of his wallet and set it on the arm of her chair. "We'll see ourselves out. Feel free to send me a text or email if calling is too much."

An hour later, Motts managed to come out of the fog of silence. Cactus hadn't moved from his sentry position in her lap. She gently ran her fingers across his head before picking up the card to her left.

Detective Inspector Teo Herceg.

Dragging the blanket off the back of her chair, Motts wrapped it around her body. She tried to shake off the feeling of embarrassment. Shutdowns in front of others always left her with an acute sense of raw humiliation.

She found herself warming to the intimidating detective who'd recognised the signs and kindly given her space to recover. Even her well-meaning mother didn't understand being alone was *exactly* what she needed during times of stress. She'd have liked Teo Herceg more if he'd answered her questions.

Despite a growing hunger, Motts couldn't make herself get up out of the chair. She'd sat through the afternoon even as the sun (and the police) disappeared. No amount of self-cajoling shifted her out of the mental funk leftover from her shutdown.

"Motts?"

"I'm here." She lifted her arm up to signal to her auntie Lily. "Shouldn't you be in the office?"

Her auntie Lily ran the Chen-Mottley Brewery in Looe with her uncle Tom. The couple had met when Motts's uncle had travelled to Singapore for a university exchange program. They'd fallen in love and eventually made their way back to Cornwall in their twenties.

"Young Hughie reached out to River. He thought you might appreciate a little comfort food." Lily lifted up the large container in her arms. "I baked this afternoon, so I figured you could share in the wealth. Chicken curry crispy pies, coconut egg tarts, and the sesame shortcake you're so fond of."

Motts got up, setting Cactus on the floor, and gave her aunt a hug. "Thank you."

"Come, come. Eat." She guided Motts towards the kitchen. "And tell me all about this handsome new detective. River said Hughie thought you seemed infatuated."

Oh, for the love of village gossip.

"I don't do infatuation. I met the man once. He seemed aesthetically pleasing, if a bit overgrown." Motts waited impatiently for her aunt to lift the lid on the container. "Thank you, Auntie."

Lily wrapped her arm around Motts's shoulders. "He might be a nice man."

FOUR DAYS AFTER THE DISCOVERY OF THE BODY, the police had finished combing every centimetre of her garden. They were gone, leaving a mess in their wake. On the plus side, the ground had essentially been turned over, and all the stones were gone, saving her a bit of time and effort.

I need my routine.

Ever since moving to Cornwall, Motts had been on a rollercoaster ride. She wanted to find stable ground. The first step was settling into her routine.

She broke her day up into three parts. Her morning was spent taking care of her beloved animals and herself. The afternoon went to business—emails and folding flowers for orders. And her evening involved catching up on YouTube videos, since she rarely watched movies or television, and reading by the fireplace.

By the following morning, Motts felt like herself again. She'd even managed to unpack the last remaining box. And more importantly, Vina, Nish, and River had come over to help her change out all the decoration in the cottage.

Vina had insisted. She thought Motts needed a home suited to a thirty-nine-year-old woman instead of a sixty-something maiden aunt. Auntie Daisy had been overly fond of antique lace and roses.

They managed to remove most of it in an evening. River had promised to take all the decorations to a charity shop. Motts didn't want to just throw everything away.

"Did you ask your mum if she wanted any of Auntie Daisy's stuff?" River had the last box in his arms. "It is her sister."

"She's not talking to me." Motts shrugged. "She thinks I'll come home to London because I can't live on my own."

Vina came over to give her a hug. "She needs to adjust. Don't they call it empty nest syndrome?"

"How can it be empty when Dad's there?" Motts

frowned at her. She was distracted by belatedly remembering something and turned to point a finger at her cousin. "Did you tell your mum a bit of gossip Hughie shared with you?"

River backed slowly towards the door. "Have to go. See you later. Bye."

CHAPTER FIVE

"Welcome to the Salty Seaman."

Motts waved awkwardly at the brown-haired man behind the counter. "Am I too early?"

Of course, you're not too early.

The welcome sign was on, and the door was open.

Why am I the way that I am?

"You're the fruit girl."

"I am *not* the fruit girl. My name is Pineapple. Call me Motts." She groaned. Why did everyone call her fruit girl? *Right, be subtle.* "Have the police contacted you?"

Bugger.

"About?" He clammed up with his lips pressed tightly together.

Motts watched him storm through the door that

led into the kitchen, leaving her to place an order with one of the other shop employees. "Can I get an order to go, please?"

With her cod fish cakes, chips with curry sauce, and battered sausage, Motts went outside and secured the packet of food in the top box on the back of her Vespa. She'd ridden over to Looe earlier to deliver a flower bouquet and on the way back caved to her sudden urge for fried food. Being able to question Rhona Walters's brother had been a bonus.

"You live up in the cottage on the hill."

Motts closed the lid on her top box and turned to find a slightly less angry man. "Yes."

"The cottage Daisy stayed in. My sister used to deliver fish and chips to her every evening and help clean up around the house. I'm Innis Walters. My wife, Rose, tells me I was rude." He didn't apologise, but Motts was too busy trying to figure out what to do with her hands to care. "You were the one who found my sister."

So it was Rhona Walters.

Motts shifted awkwardly in front of him. "Do you remember when your sister went missing?"

"She was going to London for a few days. Left a note in the shop after hours." Innis glanced over his shoulder when his wife called from inside. "Again. Sorry I was so short."

He was gone before Motts could think of another question. She made her way home quickly, trying to beat the incoming rain. The clouds opened up seconds after she ducked inside the cottage.

She was splitting her cod with Cactus when a thought occurred to her. The trip from Polperro to London, depending on the plane, train, or automobile, could be anywhere from an hour flight to over four hours in a car.

The Salty Seaman closed at eleven at night, according to the sales flyer stuck to the top of her food container. *Who leaves for London close to midnight? No one. There's no way Rhona planned to visit friends by going so late in the day.*

No way.

Well, she could've, but it's so unlikely.

And with her body in the garden, Rhona had quite obviously never made it out of Polperro. What if the killer had left the note? Did Innis still have it? Had the police tested it for fingerprints?

Slow down, Motts, you're not a copper. They're not going to answer your questions.

But it didn't hurt to ask, did it?

With her (and Cactus's lunch) finished, Motts

considered how to discover more information. She had Inspector Herceg's contact information. But Plymouth was significantly further away than Looe, and she'd already made one trip on her scooter.

Arguing back and forth with herself, Motts tried to decide on email versus text message. The inspector had seemed so understanding the day they'd met. And he had invited her to reach out to him.

She'd almost decided to text when her phone rang. She threw it across the room in surprise. *Well, that was helpful and also a complete overreaction to a sudden sound.*

By the time Motts found her phone, it had stopped ringing. The number was unfamiliar, so she decided not to call back. They hadn't left a message either.

"Do you think the inspector would be more likely to tell me about the case via text or email?" Motts swayed with Cactus in her arms while staring out at the garden. "Is purring a yes or a no? I'm never certain."

What if I just don't contact him? Then I won't have answers. But I'll be way less stressed, so that's something.

After ten minutes of pacing in front of her laptop, Motts sat down at her desk. She typed out seven versions of her email. None of the drafts seemed right, so she sent a quick text message to call for reinforcements.

Vina arrived twenty minutes later with tea and pastries from the coffee shop. She dragged a chair over to sit beside her at the table. "So, you want my help sending a message to a boy? You do realise we used to date, right?"

Motts poked her best friend in the side. "First, it's not that kind of message. Second, he's a grown man—too grown. And third, we dated until we realised we make better friends. And also, we're not compatible."

Vina clutched at her heart. "Oh, the pain. The betrayal. The hurt."

"Are you being dramatic?"

"Yes." Vina settled back into the chair. She turned her attention towards the laptop. "Okay. What are we doing? Why are you emailing the incredibly attractive detective inspector from Plymouth?"

"You haven't seen him."

"We googled him." She grinned unrepentantly at Motts, who covered her face with her hands. "Well? Why are we emailing him?"

"There was a body abandoned under stones. Just there." Motts gestured outside, almost knocking her mug of tea onto the laptop. "I slept with a decomposed body nearby. I have to know what happened to her.

What if the berk gets away with leaving her like some random bit of rubbish?"

Vina twisted in her chair and placed a hand on Motts's arm. "Is this about Jenny? Your friend who died?"

"No." Motts paused to consider her automatic denial. Jenny's disappearance had always haunted her. "Maybe?"

Vina kept her gaze on Motts for a few more seconds before turning back towards the computer. "Right. We're going to play detective. Am I Holmes or Watson? Not sure I can pull off casual disdain like Cumbersquatch."

"That's not his name." Motts shoved Vina lightly. "Think we're more Rosemary and Thyme."

"Intelligent but slightly accident-prone women who solve crimes with panache?" Vina considered for a moment. "Sounds about right."

Over tea and pastries, they considered four more drafts of the email. Vina insisted she didn't want to sound *overly* interested in the case. She finally sent a concise message sharing the conversation with Innis Walters and her odd first meeting with Danny Orchard.

She thought the detective might like to know about the Orchards' reaction to her clearing out the gardens.

They hadn't wanted her messing with the stones. Was it because they knew Rhona was buried underneath?

Was that why they'd practically abandoned her auntie's garden? Allowing it to grow wildly? Auntie Daisy hadn't mentioned anything. *I wonder if Mum knows.*

Considering her options, Motts sent a text message to her dad. Her mum hadn't shown any interest in speaking with her. Maybe he could ask her if Auntie Daisy had said anything about her garden or strange smells.

"I was wondering about the smell. Wouldn't a decomposing body pong a bit?" Vina grabbed one of the last pastries. "I'll split the last chocolate coconut curry pasty with you."

"The smell would be awful. Absolutely terrible. And it would've spread." She grabbed her portion of the sweet and savoury pasty. "How did no one else notice? My mysterious mystery masterfully muddles minds."

"Eight out of ten points." Vina gave her alliteration a thumbs up.

"I think the judges were bribed. It was clearly a 9.5 at the least." Motts hit refresh on her inbox five times. "Why hasn't he responded?"

"He's a detective inspector. And male. He probably doesn't even bother to check his emails but once a week." Vina grinned. "Want to watch *Bake Off*?"

"I don't watch telly often." Motts refreshed a few more times. "You should go home."

Vina shook her head and laughed. "Never change, Motts."

"Why would I?" She frowned at her. "I'm me."

"Figure of speech."

"Figures of speech are weird."

CHAPTER SIX

Two days went by without Motts hearing back from the detective. She didn't know whether to take his lack of response personally or not. He did have other cases to work on, surely.

When the anxiety began to stress her too much, Motts decided to take advantage of the beautifully sunny weather. It had warmed up ever so slightly. She put Cactus in his sun-protection shirt and allowed him to meander around for a little while.

Mostly, Cactus stayed nearby. She turned her attention to gathering up all the trampled weeds and plants the police investigation had left behind. A scratching sound across the garden drew her attention.

"What did you find?" Motts glanced around to

find Cactus investigating part of the fencing around the edge of the garden. "We don't scratch wood."

That sounds slightly obscene.

Crouching down on the ground, Motts found Cactus had become interested in a tiny carving. She couldn't recall having seen it before. But from the little mound of dirt, she wondered if it had been hidden.

On the inside post, Motts traced the lines of a heart and two initials—RW and DO. *Wait. Rhona Walters and Danny Orchard? Could it really be them?*

Were they dating?

No one had mentioned that to her. Motts sent a text to Vina and Nish to ask if either of them knew about the two dating. She also took a photo with her phone before lifting Cactus into her arms.

Rhona Walters and Danny Orchard.

Interesting.

Heading into the cottage, Motts fed both of her pets. She watched Moss munch away on a piece of fruit for several minutes while pondering the new layer of intrigue. *Who can I ask about Rhona's dating life without causing a fuss?*

Her most recent project caught her attention. She'd created a quilled peacock from long strips of deep blue, forest green, shimmering gold, and vibrant violet paper. It had taken her hours to first sketch the outline, then carefully glue down scrolled strips, one after the other.

Quilling wasn't her favourite form of art. Motts preferred origami, but she did offer the intricate pieces on commission. Marnie had wanted the large peacock for her shop; she'd even given her a shadow box created out of reclaimed wood.

Picking up the shadow box, Motts decided to make the delivery a day early. With the number of people coming in and out of a bridal shop, Marnie might remember who Rhona had dated. Neither Vina nor Nish had known the woman well enough to say.

They'd also been living in London at the time Rhona had gone missing.

Stepping outside, Motts breathed the lovely fresh air blowing in off the sea. She carefully secured the frame onto her scooter. And then she paused to glance down the street to her magnificent view of the harbour.

I love Cornwall.

Hopping on her scooter, Motts could almost imagine she was riding a Vespa along the Amalfi Coast. She cautiously rode down the winding road that led from her cottage through the holiday homes into the village. Marnie's shop was in the middle of a row of shops on Lansallos Street.

She stopped at the last corner on the downhill,

checking both ways before pulling out onto the road. A screech of tires was her only warning before a Golf GT raced out from between two buildings and collided with her back tire. Her Vespa went skidding on its side, and the picture frame went into a nearby cottage wall with a glass-breaking thud.

Motts rolled along the ground into the hedge on the opposite side of her poor scooter. She grunted in pain. The world went from a chaotic rush of sound and sensation to an eerie stillness, as though she'd gone through a category five typhoon in the space of a minute. *What the hell happened?*

A second round of squealing tires and the harsh rev of an engine had her attempting to roll further into the hedge. The vehicle flew by her so closely, it ruffled her hair. She heard a door open, and some rather colourful shouting followed.

Motts tried to gently test her body for injuries. Her arms and legs hurt but moved fine. She didn't think anything had broken. "Did anyone get the number of the bus that ran me over?"

"Don't move, love."

She opened her eyes, blinking at the blood trickling down from a cut above her left eyebrow. "The hedge is scratchy."

"Stay still."

Motts tilted her head slightly to see an older gentleman kneeling beside her in the muddy grass. He had his mobile pressed to his ear. "I'm alright."

"Not so sure, dear. Why don't you stay put until the ambulance arrives to make certain? Okay?" He patted her hand gingerly. "I've got a CCTV camera on the front of my cottage. I'll let the police have it. The young bastard won't get away with it."

"Young?"

"Can't imagine an older person driving one of those wind-up toy cars. I'm Caradoc Ferris. Most people call me Doc." He kept a hold of her hand. "The lady on the phone wants to know if you're feeling any pain."

"I went off my scooter into a hedge. Pain is definitely on the list of things I'm feeling." Motts eased herself along the ground out from under the hedge. "I didn't break anything."

Aside from my scooter, my pride, and my peacock.

From her position in the ditch, Motts couldn't really see much other than the sky, the kind gentleman holding her hand, and the hedge. She heard vehicles and chatter from the gathering onlookers. Running footsteps caught her attention above everything else.

"Motts?"

"Nish?" She canted her head towards him,

ignoring the grumblings from Doc about not moving before the medics arrived. "I'm okay."

"I doubt it." He knelt next to Doc. "Want my AirPods? I've got my Bollywood playlist on at the moment. It might help drown out all the excess noise."

"Can you see if my peacock is broken?" Motts tilted her head from side to side to allow Nish to place the AirPods in her ears. "Think it flew off and hit the kerb or a cottage. Maybe both. Marnie's going to be upset."

"I'll take care of your things. I promise. Vina's on her way. We'll follow you wherever the ambulance takes you. I have no doubt they're taking you to a hospital." Nish glanced behind him when sirens grew closer. "Hughie's here as well. Just think how exciting this will be. You'll get to fly in a helicopter."

"I'm okay, Nish."

"No, you aren't." He shifted out of the way when the paramedics came racing towards them. "Want me to tell them you're autistic?"

"You literally just did. The inane inquiry is insulting."

"The judges give you an eight out of ten for the alliteration." Nish smiled, but she thought it seemed a little strained. "The *i*'s have it."

Once the air ambulance crew checked her over,

they insisted on taking her to the hospital in Plymouth. It was the nearest full accident and emergency department in the area. They were concerned about a possible head injury, given the severity of the impact.

The next hour went by in a strange blur. Motts didn't recall answering questions, though she knew the paramedics had asked them. She found herself bundled up on a stretcher and rushed to Plymouth.

Given the small nature of the villages in Cornwall, Motts wasn't surprised the nearest large hospital required either a fifty-minute drive or a short helicopter ride. She greatly appreciated the fantastic work the air ambulance did. They'd taken great care of her.

By the time Motts had been moved to a private room, she'd mostly recovered from the shock of the hit-and-run. She sat with her arms folded, trying not to touch the hospital sheets. They had a texture that drove her batty. "What in the world just happened?"

She wasn't alone for a long. A familiar figure slipped through the door. "Hello."

"Ms Mottley? Mind if I sit with you?"

"Motts, please." Motts found herself grateful for the distraction that came in the form of Detective Inspector Herceg. She waved him towards the nearby chair. "Why are you here?"

He grabbed a chair from against the wall and

placed it next to the bed. "Constable Stone is on his way up with your friends. They'll be here soon. They got stuck in traffic."

Motts stared when he held out a small pack of Jaffa Cakes. "Not sure this is hospital approved."

"Your friend Pravina thought you might need comfort food." Inspector Herceg placed the packet on the bed beside her. "Are you up to a few questions?"

"I'm a captive audience at the moment." Motts was still waiting for her doctor to return. She had a feeling they'd be letting her head home, since none of her injuries were severe. "What did you want to know?"

"Can you remember the incident?"

"Accident, you mean?" Motts asked. She didn't like it when people used the wrong words. Incident sounded serious—intentional. "Was the other driver found?"

"Not yet." Inspector Herceg cleared his throat and sighed deeply. "I've seen the CCTV footage. Constable Stone managed to email it over to me. The driver had been sitting in his vehicle for over an hour until you came into view. From down the hill, they could easily see you leaving the cottage."

Motts frowned at the detective. "Incident, not accident. You think they were waiting for me? Or watching me?"

"Possibly both." He slipped a notebook out of his jacket pocket. "Tell me about your day."

Picking at the opening on the Jaffa Cakes packet, Motts took the inspector through her day. She skipped her morning routine. He didn't need to know how she did the same thing almost every day or how she brushed her teeth.

Did he?

No.

Her recollection of the crash itself was fuzzy. Motts vaguely remembered seeing the vehicle moving towards her. She didn't remember skidding across the ground or hitting the hedge.

Inspector Herceg actually reached out a hand towards her, then pulled back when her voice shook during the recounting of her injuries. "We'll locate the driver of the vehicle."

"Golf GT. I recognised the make. Vina used to have one during our university days." Motts stared down at the biscuit packet. "You didn't need that information."

"I'll.... Hold on a second." He grabbed his phone from his pocket when it beeped, reading the text before balancing it on his leg. "Your friends are going to be a few more minutes. Why don't I wait with you?"

"If you want." She decided to open up the box,

taking one of the chocolate-covered cakes for herself and offering him the packet. "Why would someone try to run me over? Maybe they didn't see me."

Inspector Herceg waved off the offer of a Jaffa cake. "The thought occurred to me that you found a body in your garden. I'll have more than a few questions for the driver about not only this incident but your discovery."

"But I don't know anything about Rhona's death."

"If the two incidents are related, the killer might not know that." He reached out for a second time to squeeze her hand. "I'll be asking Constable Stone to keep a close eye on you until we have the driver in custody."

"I'm fine."

"I'm confident you will be."

CHAPTER SEVEN

"Do you need another pillow?" Vina had two large decorative cushions in her arms. "Maybe to prop up your leg?"

"You've brought me twenty. How many do you think I need?" Motts had settled on the couch facing the window out to the garden. "Did you raid Ikea? Do we have one?"

"As much as I adore you, I'm not driving to Exeter for pillows. Amma has an unhealthy obsession with cushions. I borrowed them." Vina squashed them beside her. "Are you sure you don't need anything?"

"Vina."

She shot across the living room to sit beside Motts, wrapping her arms gently around her. "Do you know how bloody terrifying it was seeing you on the ground?

Your scooter in pieces. Blood on your face. I didn't know how badly you'd been hurt."

"I'm okay."

And she was. The doctors had released her from the hospital within a few hours. Her only injuries were scrapes and bruises. She knew her body would be sore for several days.

It could've been so much worse, though.

"Hughie said they found the vehicle abandoned down the street. It was stolen." Vina returned to her chair. "They didn't get a glimpse of the driver's face. They're trying to see if they find fingerprints."

"Hughie told you all of that?" Motts was surprised the constable had been so forthcoming.

"Well, told is a strong word. I might've overheard a conversation while he was in line at the coffee shop." Vina preened. "I *am* a genius."

"Sneaky."

"A sneaky genius." She stretched her arm out to grab her tablet on the coffee table. "Nish said your parents are coming to visit."

"I tried to block out the memory of their call." Motts had mixed feelings about her parents' imminent arrival. She loved them but having her space to herself had been fantastic. It showed her how stifling life in

London had become. "Not sure why they're coming. I'm fine."

"Someone tried to run you over, Motts. They weren't messing around." Vina set her tablet down on her lap. "Your parents love you. Of course, they're going to make the trip from London to see you're okay. A phone call isn't the same."

"I could Skype."

"Video calls aren't the same as in person. It's a neurotypical thing, Mottsy. We need to see with our own eyes when we're worried about someone we love." Vina had often over the years of their friendship and dating proved to be a brilliant non-autistic translator when Motts needed. "Amma and Nish gave me a few days off from the shop. I'll play buffer for you."

Motts didn't know how to respond, so she went with the first thought in her mind. "Can you make tea?"

With a wry chuckle, Vina headed into the kitchen. Motts focused on petting Cactus and watching the birds in the garden. She never knew how to respond to the kindness of other people.

It was almost as bad as compliments. Other people seemed to manage gracefully. Motts always felt so incredibly awkward in comparison.

"Motts? Why is there a bowl of pineapple in your

fridge? You never eat pineapple." Vina brought the dish into the living room. "I don't think I've ever seen you try it."

"Detective Inspector Herceg sent me a fruit basket. All pineapple." Motts had been stunned by the delivery. Hughie had brought it to her with a note from the inspector. "I think it was a joke?"

"I'm sorry. Hold on. I need a moment to process the bizarre turn of this conversation." Vina sat down on the arm of the sofa. "Detective Inspector Tall, Handsome, and Brooding sent you a bowl of pineapple. You. Sent you pineapple."

"Are you asking for clarification or mocking my pineapple?"

"He sent pineapple to Pineapple." Vina clutched the bowl in her arms. "He has a sense of humour. Who knew?"

"Do you want the fruit?"

"And deprive you of your namesake?" She waved the bowl under Motts's nose. "Did you send a thank-you email?"

"Text." Motts hadn't known how to respond to the surprise gift. She figured a short "thanks" worked well enough. "I said thank you."

"That's all?" Vina shook her head dramatically. "I've got to work on your flirting."

"I don't want to flirt."

"You're hopeless."

"Says my ex-girlfriend." Motts blocked the bowl when Vina waved it at her a second time. "The kettle is whistling."

"Saved by the boiling water." She went back to the kitchen.

Despite the incessant teasing, Motts was grateful to have Vina in her life. She didn't know anyone else who understood her so well. They hadn't worked as a couple, but at least it hadn't ruined their friendship.

She still remembered the uncomfortably awful break-up conversation. They'd realised over time that neither of their needs were being met. Vina wanted a sexual relationship that Motts, as someone who was asexual, couldn't provide.

They'd remained the best of friends. Motts had a feeling her life would be quite dull without the vibrant and extroverted Vina. Nish, thankfully, played a calm counterpart to his sister.

"Tea." Vina appeared beside her, breaking Motts out of her thoughts. "I couldn't find the Jaffa Cakes. Did you hide them?"

"If I don't, my dad will eat all of them when they arrive." Motts hated the impending intrusion into her space. She'd only just made the cottage home, and her parents tended to take over like an invasive vine in a flower garden. *I need a distraction before I worry myself into an anxiety attack.* "Did Hughie have any other information about the driver?"

"Nope. But, I have gossip for you." Vina retreated to the sofa across from Motts. She curled up with her legs crossed and a blanket wrapped around her shoulders. "My Amma is a genius who could get a stone to give up its secrets. She chatted with Rose Walters when she came to pick up bread. Apparently, you were right. Rhona had been seeing Danny in secret. They'd kept their relationship quiet because Danny had a jealous ex-girlfriend."

"Did he?" Motts wondered how jealous the former girlfriend had been. "Was she actually jealous? Or was he making claims to inflate his ego?"

"Amma didn't find out. She thought Rose was getting suspicious about her questions." Vina tapped the side of her mug. "Nish remembers Danny in secondary school. He dated several girls. But I remember him being single for a while when we came back from university. I don't think he had a jealous ex."

"Okay?"

"But Rhona had an overprotective brother. *And* Dad remembered when their father died and the business went to her and Innis. They fought a lot, because she didn't want to run the fish and chip shop." Vina grabbed her phone and glanced at it. "Nish wants to know if we're hungry. He's making a lamb biryani pizza."

"Tell him I'll trade him pineapple for a few slices."

"He might not understand that text." She grinned. "*Vina*."

"Do you honestly want me to text him that we'll trade *pineapple* for pizza. Your *name* is Pineapple." Vina's shoulders shook while she laughed. "I'll stick with a simple yes and hurry the hell up."

Over a dinner of pizza and beer, the trio considered the accident and their casual investigation. The twins stayed into the evening. Motts appreciated their support when her parents arrived after ten o'clock.

Thankfully for everyone involved, her parents were tired enough not to stay up late. Motts left them to the master bedroom. She stayed in the guest room with Cactus for company.

The following morning, Motts tried not to lose her mind. Her mum had insisted on making breakfast despite Motts and her dad only eating toast. Cactus had appreciated the sausage.

"I might hide in the shed." Motts had Cactus in his sun-shirt on a leash. They were making a circuit in the garden to avoid her parents for at least a few minutes.

"I'm glad we have one. It gives us somewhere to stay until they go home."

Meow.

"Exactly. She hasn't been here a day, and my fridge is completely rearranged. Illogically rearranged. What if I *need* my butter on the middle shelf? Not her kitchen." She rubbed her nose against his downy fuzz. "Why does it matter?"

Meow.

"Poppet?" Her dad stood nearby with a mug in his hands. "Your mum is driving out to see your auntie Lily in Looe. Want to go? Think they're going shopping."

"No."

"Thought so. She already left." He winked at her. "Why don't we pop down to the shops ourselves? Grab a coffee and something a little sweeter than the toast we had for breakfast. You can tell me all about your new young man."

"What new young man?" Motts didn't move from her post, allowing Cactus to meander around a little longer. "No new young man. No man. Well, there are men. I don't have one."

"New woman?"

"No new people." She picked Cactus up to carry him inside. "Why?"

"Your mum had a call with your auntie Lily. And she thought you'd become friendly with some detective inspector." Her dad followed her into the cottage. "Poppet?"

Setting Cactus onto his favourite spot on the couch, Motts made sure to check on Moss and feed both of them. She cleaned up the dishes while her dad waited patiently for her to respond. And she had no intention of doing so.

Why is everyone always so obsessed with whether I'm dating someone?

She finished the last of the dishes and ran out of things to delay the rest of the conversation. "Are we walking? Not sure you'd fit on my bicycle, and I haven't replaced my scooter."

Nish and Hughie had kindly gathered up all the parts of her poor Vespa. There hadn't been much of a point. The local mechanic had taken all of a second to declare it unfixable.

She didn't want to get a new one. The old one had been perfect. She'd been used to driving it, and salespeople intimidated her.

"We'll find you a new one," he promised. "Let's walk. The air and exercise will be good for us. Are you recovered enough?"

"Yes." Motts grabbed her cardigan from the

coatrack by the door. "I'm okay. The bruises make everything seem more dramatic."

Her dad shook his head. "When you were six, you broke your wrist. You kept insisting nothing hurt. A broken wrist and it didn't hurt. You'll forgive me if I don't take your word for how injured you were after a car tried to kill you."

Well, when he puts it like that.

"I'm okay to walk into the village." Motts looped her arm around her dad's. She leaned her head against his arm. "I'm glad you came to visit."

"But wish I'd left your mum at home?"

"I love Mum," Motts insisted.

"She means well, poppet. It's not always easy to see your child all grown up and out on their own." He kissed the top of her head. "Give her time to adjust."

"I'm almost forty." Motts didn't understand why her mum kept trying to treat her like a child. "She wasn't this bad in London."

"You didn't notice it in London." He patted her hand gently. "She'll come around. Don't worry."

CHAPTER EIGHT

Motts rushed around the corner with a package held tightly in her arms. She had her head down and wound up running straight into someone coming in the opposite direction. "Bugger. I'm so sorry."

Detective Inspector Herceg reached out to grab her by the arms to steady her. "Are you alright?"

"Fine."

"Kernow Chocolate." He read the name on the logo covering all four sides of the box. "Are you a fan?"

"The thirty bars inside are *definitely* proof I'm more than a fan." She hefted the package up in her arms. "They've got a new one—a Cherry Bakewell Tart bar. I'm dying to try it."

"I'm partial to the Banoffee and Cream Tea." He frowned at her. "Can I carry the box for you?"

"As long as you don't run off with my chocolate." Motts allowed him to take the package out of her arms. "I'm going to have to replace my scooter. It's a nightmare lugging anything up the hill without it."

Three days had passed since her accident. Her parents had left for London the day before; they both had to return to work. She was still putting things in the cottage back the way she wanted.

Her mum might mean well, but rearranging furniture and everything else made Motts uneasy. She needed her personal space to be set up for her comfort. Not her parents'. She didn't think her mum would ever wholly understand.

She'd at least begun to speak to Motts again. It had only taken one near-death experience. They'd gone a long way to repairing their relationship, much to her dad's relief.

"Why don't I give you a lift?"

"Aren't you supposed to be doing inspectoring-type things?"

"Is 'inspectoring' a word?" He placed her package carefully into the back seat of his car and motioned for her to get into the passenger side. "I already had my interview with Innis Walters."

"Are you arresting him?"

"Not today."

Motts narrowed her eyes on the detective. She didn't know if not today meant not at all or not just yet. "Have you questioned Danny Orchard?"

He paused while starting the vehicle to gaze at her. "He's admitted to dating Rhona briefly. He claimed they weren't serious."

"Serious enough to carve their initials into my fence," Motts pointed out.

"Ah, but we can't prove who defaced your property." He eased the car out of the parking space. "Are you investigating for me?"

"No," she answered sharply. "I wouldn't."

"Of course."

Deciding silence was the safest bet, Motts stared out the window. She waved to Marnie when they passed the bridal shop. *Brilliant.* She had no doubts local gossip would start spreading rumours about her catching a lift with the detective.

Detective Inspector Herceg seemed content to be quiet all the way until he'd carried her box into the cottage. He set the package on the table. "Constable Stone hasn't seen anyone around your cottage. He's eased off his watch. It's possible the hit-and-run driver thinks you got their message. Whatever it was supposed to be. If you see anyone suspicious, don't hesitate to call 999 immediately."

"I'm sure it was an accident," Motts lied. She thought the killer was trying to send her a message. "I'm not worried."

Another lie.

"Want help opening your package?"

"No." Motts grabbed scissors from the coffee table. She'd used them to work on repairing Marnie's peacock. "Would you like one of the bars? I did order an excessive amount."

"No such thing." He placed a hand on the box to keep it steady while she cut the tape. "I wouldn't want to deprive you."

"I'm apparently an emotional shopper. And a stress shopper. And a shopper when my mum comes to visit and rearranges my entire house for no reason." Motts took a deep breath and smiled apologetically at the detective. "I bought a lot of chocolate."

"Can't say I blame you. Kernow has the best I've tried." He hesitantly took the bar of Cream Tea Milk Chocolate. He slipped it into the inside pocket of his coat. "Thank you."

"Don't you want it?" Motts had already begun unwrapping one of the six bars of Bakewell Tart Milk

Chocolate she'd purchased. It was her favourite. "It's delicious."

"I'm going to save it for my knitting group. We always pool our snack resources." Detective Inspector Herceg shook his head when she went to offer him a chunk of hers. "I couldn't."

Motts shrugged. Fair enough. She wasn't going to force her chocolate on someone. "More for me. Wait. Did you say you had a knitting group?"

He scratched the stubble on his jaw for a second and finally nodded. "I find it relaxing. My baka taught me."

"Baka?"

"My grandmother. She still lives in Dubrovnik. She didn't want to move when my parents came. Stubborn." He sighed. "We used to knit together. Police work isn't for the fainthearted, particularly cold cases. My small group meets twice a month."

Motts couldn't help staring at his hands. The detective was a large man. He had to be at least six-foot-five, with broad shoulders and body to match; his fingers weren't exactly slender. "You don't seem like a knitter."

He eased his phone out of his pocket and after a few seconds turned it around to show a beautiful dark navy-coloured scarf. "My latest project."

"The knitting detective sounds like one of those cosy mysteries my gran reads." Motts sat on her arm of the chair, munching on her chocolate bar. "Did you talk to Innis about his running the store with his sister? They apparently argued quite a bit about her lack of interest while having 51 percent ownership."

"Ms Mottley."

"Motts," she interrupted.

"Alright, Motts it is." He stepped closer to her. His brow creased in what she assumed was worry; she never completely grasped facial expressions. "Why don't you let me ask the questions and investigate? We don't want anyone trying to run you over for a second time."

"Accident."

"Neither of us believes that," he said confidently. "I'll be leaving."

"Thanks for the lift, Detective."

"Teo." He waved off her thanks with a smile. She liked the way his brown eyes twinkled when he grinned. "If anyone bothers you at all, call me."

"Good luck with your knitting." Motts carefully folded the wrapper around her half-eaten bar of chocolate. "It's a fun hobby. I tried once, but the texture of yarn drove me batty within a few minutes."

And it had. Motts had thrown the entire ball of

yarn out the window during a meltdown. Her mum had stopped trying to force new hobbies on her, so the exercise hadn't been a complete waste of time.

"Stay safe. Make sure you lock up after me." Teo saw himself out, petting Cactus on the way.

Motts watched the detective leave through the front window. He waved before backing down the path to the road. She bent down to allow Cactus into her arms. "He's very aesthetically pleasing."

Meow.

"Yes, he does have a strange hobby for a detective. I like it. Makes him less intimidating." Motts wandered through the cottage, bending down to stoke the fire. "I've no idea how Auntie Daisy managed during the winter. It's absolutely freezing up on this hill."

Meow.

"It's too early for your snack." She placed him gently on the mound of blankets near the back window. Cactus greatly enjoyed watching all the activity in the garden. "Well, these paper violets aren't going to make themselves, are they?"

CHAPTER NINE

The following day, Motts wrapped up her second attempt at the peacock. The scrolled papers hadn't been damaged severely. She had needed to reframe the artwork; River had driven down to Looe to grab one at an antique shop.

He'd also gone out with her to pick up a new scooter. She'd managed to find an exact replacement for her old one. *Why mess with a good thing?*

Staring at the scooter, Motts didn't quite feel up to driving for a second time with the peacock strapped to the back. She decided to struggle down the long, narrow stone steps leading from her street into the village. By the time she arrived at Marnie's shop, her arms were about ready to fall off.

"Why didn't you call? My Perry could've easily given you a lift. Or had Hughie pick you up in his patrol car." Marnie held the door open for her. "Are you feeling better, love? Aside from exhausted by the exertion?"

Exhausted exertion exhausts everyone.

Don't alliterate out loud.

Motts gingerly set down the fixed peacock on the counter in the bridal shop. She shifted awkwardly while Marnie oohed and ahhed over her creation. "I had to use a different frame. Sorry. They couldn't fix the other one."

"I'm just glad they could fix you." Marnie placed the quilled peacock on the wall behind the counter. "How absolutely lovely. You're so talented."

She didn't know how to respond, so she ignored the compliment. "I'll have the violet bouquets ready by the end of the week for you."

"No rush, dear. The bride isn't coming in for her fitting for another month. She'll adore your paper bouquet. She'd been devastated at not having flowers because of her husband-to-be's allergies. Your paper treasures are a lifesaver for her." Marnie came around the counter to give her a warm hug. Motts told herself not to stiffen up; non-autistics always seemed mildly insulted if you cringed at their touch. "Now, why don't you grab yourself lunch? I'm about to close shop myself for a quick bite to eat."

Once outside in the bright sunshine, Motts considered her options. She thought about heading down to the sandwich bar or grabbing something from Griffin Brews. But her feet led her down the street towards the Salty Seaman.

"Fish cakes, again?" Innis glanced up when she stepped inside.

"Cod and chips, please." Motts twisted her wallet around in her hands. She watched him gathering up the chips. "It must be lovely, running a shop with such a rich family history."

"Lovely." Innis sniffed.

She gripped her wallet tightly. He didn't exactly sound as though it was lovely. "Did Rhona enjoy spending time here with you?"

"Bint didn't want to get her fingers greasy." He banged the packet of chips on the counter. "Why don't you keep your nose away before it gets burnt? Hmm?"

Motts winced at the slightly smashed chips shoved at her. "Can I get a battered sausage as well?"

"Fine." Innis snatched the chips back, tossing them in the rubbish. "I'll get you fresh ones."

While Innis gathered her meal up for a second time, Motts tried to find a subtle way to ask another question. She couldn't shake the feeling he knew more about his sister's disappearance. Innis banged around in his small kitchen area.

Do you have a controlling interest in the shop?

That sounds ridiculous. He's not an investor. He didn't even want to talk about whether she enjoyed the job.

"Did Rhona want to do something else with her life?"

"Sure. She wanted to swan down the runway in Paris." Innis snorted viciously. "Take your questions and your fish and bugger off."

"Sorry." Motts had her money thrown in her face when she offered it. She muttered sorry all the way out of the chip shop. Her hands clutched tightly around the paper packet. "That went brilliantly."

Her fingers trembled around her lunch. She loathed confrontation. It made her want to hide inside a cupboard for a month.

The stairs up to her cottage seemed to have grown by at least thirty by the time Motts made it home. She rushed inside and leaned heavily against the closed door. *Right. Maybe I should leave the questions to the police.*

Or find a way to ask them from a distance.

Meow.

She dodged around Cactus to set the food on the table. Her cat hopped up next to it. He poked a paw at the paper. "You can't have a chip before I do. Rude. Didn't your mother teach you any manners?"

I'm his mum.

Grabbing ketchup from the fridge, Motts squeezed a generous amount on the chips. She wondered why Innis had been so instantly angry at her question. It had been the least offensive to her mind.

Why was he so testy about the subject?

Meow.

"It was suspicious, Cactus. You read my mind. Good boy." Motts picked a flake of cod for her finicky feline. "Why would he want to get rid of his sister? For complete control of the business? Do fish and chip shops make that much money?"

Maybe Innis hadn't appreciated putting in all the effort and having to share the money. Motts knew from watching crime shows that money and sex tended to be the biggest motivators for murder. She'd never understood the latter.

How is sex motivating?

It's moist. And the sounds are awful. And it takes effort.

Just. No.

Motts shuddered. Cactus sidled up to her, sniffing at the remaining fish. "You've had a snack."

Meow.

"The vet might accuse me of overfeeding you." She peeled off a few more flakes for Cactus, despite her comment. She couldn't resist his plaintive meow. "Emotionally manipulative cat."

Finishing up her lunch, Motts grabbed her laptop from the table and went over to the chair by the living room window. She turned on one of her favourite YouTubers, NerdECrafter. With the video playing in the background, she typed out a few questions in a blank document.

Who had control of the Salty Seaman? Was Innis truly angry with his sister? Did he know about her romance with Danny?

Was there actually a romance with Danny?

And why were the Orchards so interested in changes in the garden? Did they know about the body? Was Danny the one driving the vehicle?

Purr.

"Yes, I have more questions than answers." Motts shifted to the side to allow Cactus to curl up next to her. "How can I ask Innis if he resorts to shouting and slamming things around?"

When the video finished, Motts saved the file with

her questions. She decided to take advantage of the weather and go outside into the garden. Cactus seemed quite content to stay burrowed into his blanket.

The garden had been almost completely stripped bare to grass and dirt in the one section cordoned off for planting. She had a variety of herbs in little compostable pots in the cottage ready to go into the ground when it warmed up a little. There was more to do before that point, though.

For now, Motts wanted to finish laying bricks on the path going through the centre of the yard. Hughie had found them for her. She'd spent a few minutes each day extending it.

Everything in the garden was far less overwhelming when taken a bit at a time. Motts had to limit her exposure to the glorious spring air. She didn't fancy an allergy attack in the middle of February.

After ten minutes of setting down bricks, Motts moved on to putting up her bird feeder. She'd decided to use a spare fence post. Spade in hand, she went to a corner of the yard to dig a hole deep enough to secure it.

"What in the...." Motts trailed off, confused when a distinctly metallic ting sounded. Her spade had struck something *not* dirt or stone. She reached hesitantly into the hole and retrieved a small biscuit tin. "Can't I have one day outside without discovering something bizarre?"

What is this?

She had to use her fingernail to pry the lid off the rusted tin. It contained photos, multiple printed images of Danny and Rhona together, and a collection of jewellery. She found a chunky gold bracelet with an anchor charm underneath them along with a single primrose earring and a necklace.

How odd.

Motts gently untangled the earring from a sterling silver chain that had been broken. "Why would someone bury this in Auntie Daisy's garden? It's not exactly a time capsule. These aren't treasures."

In the corner of the tin, Motts noticed a collection of crushed flowers. She didn't recognise them. *Should I call Detective Inspector Herceg?*

Teo.

He said to call him Teo.

Motts brushed her dirt-covered fingers off on her jeans. She grabbed her mobile phone and contemplated what to do. "I could always text him."

Texting was safe. She didn't risk stumbling over her words or getting confused. Calling was harder when she often struggled to process what someone was saying.

One could only ask someone to repeat themselves so many times.

In the end, Motts texted Teo. She sent him an image of the contents of the tin. He told her not to move anything and to wait for Inspector Ash to come and retrieve her find.

He won't notice if I photograph everything, will he?

Motts quickly used her phone to get photos of all the individual items in the tin. She knew Marnie's husband wouldn't take long to arrive. The village wasn't a large one, after all. "Is Rhona wearing a necklace in that image?"

Jogging quickly into the cottage, Motts grabbed a magnifying glass from a drawer. She grabbed one of the close-ups of Danny and Rhona. She appeared to be wearing a delicate chain around her neck with some sort of locket.

And earrings.

Primrose earrings.

Now, why would someone have buried a tin with Rhona's jewellery, images of her and Danny, and a bloke's bracelet?

And where's the other earring?

They didn't find it with the body.

"Ms Mottley?"

"In the garden," Motts called out. She'd continued inspecting the images with her magnifying glass, trying to find any sort of clue. "Sorry to call you out here."

"Saved me from losing ten quid to Hughie on an ill-advised game of Uno." He cracked a smile that faded away when he saw her magnifying glass. "Now, I thought you weren't supposed to be investigating."

"There's a strange dried flower or herb in the tin. I was trying to identify it. For botany purposes," Motts insisted. She resisted the childish urge to cross her fingers behind her back. *Lying liars lie lazily.* "Forensics might be able to identify it. Think it's some sort of floral, as its making my nose twinge."

"Ms Mottley."

"Motts."

"Ms Mottley. Please don't draw attention to yourself by getting involved in this cold case. My Marnie wouldn't forgive me if you got hurt. She considers you a friend." Inspector Ash pulled on a pair of gloves and plucked an evidence bag out of his jacket pocket. "Is this everything you found?"

"Everything in the tin. I didn't think to go deeper in the hole." Motts tucked her hands into her pockets when the breeze off the sea picked up. "Will you tell me if they identify the flower? I might be able to say if it came from Auntie Daisy's garden."

He paused while rooting around in the hole she'd dug. "We'll see what DI Herceg thinks. Not seeing anything else here. You're fine to finish up what you were doing."

"Birdfeeder." Motts grabbed the fence post and allowed the detective to help her secure it. "Thanks."

"Storm's going to blow up." Inspector Ash got to his feet, brushing off the dirt and pulling off his gloves. He held the bag loosely in his left hand. "You should head inside. It'll come up fast."

"Alright." Motts watched him leave through the garden gate. She filled the bird feeder with seed, then took the bag and her spade to put away into her little shed. "How did Auntie Daisy not notice someone burying things right behind the cottage?"

Stepping inside the shed, Motts moved toward the back. She set the bag of seed on a shelf and stored the spade with the other tools. The door slammed behind her suddenly, scaring her half to death.

Stupid wind.

She used her phone to light the dark space and went to push at the door, only to find it stuck. "Oh, for goodness sake. Could I have one non-dramatic day? I should've stayed in London."

No, I shouldn't. It's lovely here. I won't let a few unexpected, odd moments ruin the loveliness of having a home all to myself.

I will not panic.

I won't.

Motts threw herself at the door but bounced off the hardwood with a grunt of pain. "Not my smartest move. Oh my god. What if they've gone into the cottage? Bugger. I will gut anyone with scissors if they hurt my babies."

For the second time in a month, Motts had to wait for rescue to come after a 999 call. She wasn't entirely surprised to find Inspector Ash opening the door a few minutes later. He'd barely had time to make his way down the hill.

"Are you alright?" He watched in consternation as she rushed out of the shed, ignoring him, and went straight into the cottage. "Ms Mottley."

She collapsed on the couch with a disgruntled Cactus. "I imagined all kinds of terrible things happening. I don't know how the wind managed to slam the door so I got locked into the shed."

"It didn't." Inspector Ash held up a piece of wood; he once again had gloves on his hand. "I found this blocking the exit."

"Oh." Motts blinked away the tears gathering in

the corners of her eyes. She didn't understand why someone would lock her in the shed—and how had they gotten by the detective. "Oh."

He crouched by the sofa, seeming a lot less stoic and scary than when she'd first seen him. "I'm going to call my Marnie. She can bring tea and cakes. I think you might not want to be by yourself for too long."

"I'm alright."

"We're a small village, Motts. We take care of each other. She'll bring your Griffin twins as well. Troublesome duo that they are." Inspector Ash stood up and headed toward the door. "I'll just put this bit of wood in my car."

Mum and Dad are going to lose their minds if they hear about this.

We'll leave it out of the weekly family email.

A tiny lie by omission never hurt anyone.

CHAPTER TEN

Motts had never had a girls' night in—or out. She didn't know what to think when Marnie, Vina, Nish, and River all gathered in her cottage. *It's more a boys and girls quiet party.* "Don't let Cactus bully you into feeding him snacks."

"Who, me?" Nish paused with a treat bag in his hand. "No bullying required."

"Forget your sneaky, naked feline," Vina interrupted. She took a sip of her wine. "Show us the photos of what you found."

"Cactus isn't naked. He has downy fuzz all over him like a suede bodysuit." Motts carried a platter into the living room to set on the coffee table. They'd convened there by the fire to enjoy the warmth and snack on the food brought from the bakery. "Let me get this settled. Patience, Pravina."

"Patience isn't in her vocabulary." Nish dodged the smack his twin tried to aim at his head. He leaned toward Motts after she'd settled on a cushion on the carpet by the table. "Are you sure you're okay? Do you need quiet?"

"I don't know." Motts shrugged. She'd felt discombobulated by the entire experience. "Tea and snacks will help."

"Snacks always help." He pushed one of the plates closer to her. "Now what's this about a tin in the garden?"

"And don't worry. I know how to keep secrets from the inspector." Marnie winked at her. "Don't forget the apple cake. We lucked out, since I'd made this yesterday and had it ready to be eaten."

While they ate their way through the various treats, Motts transferred the images from her phone to her laptop. The wider screen made it easier for everyone to see. They all leaned forward to get a better view of the images of Rhona and Danny getting cosy with each other.

"Can you zoom in on the bracelet?" Marnie asked when Motts had flipped to the rest of the photos. She made the chunky jewellery larger. "I know I've seen someone in the village with a similar one. But I can't place it."

"How about this?" Motts slid the computer closer to the bridal shop owner.

"I know I've seen it." Marnie tapped her fingers against the top of the table. "Not Danny, but one of his friends. There was a gang of them for several years while they went to secondary school. Always causing trouble. Poor Hughie and Perry had a devil of a time getting them under control. Out at all hours, drinking their weight in whatever cheap liquor, and vandalising anything in their path."

"Danny, Noel, Eddie, Taj." Nish counted off several more names on his fingers. "They were several years behind us in school. Right bastards, all of them. I stopped them from picking on younger kids a lot. Vina had them terrified."

Vina grinned menacingly. "I threatened to carve their family jewels out with a rusted knife if they ever harassed another girl in school ever again. Danny wasn't the worst of the lot, but he never stopped his friends either."

"Are you sure the bracelet isn't Danny's?" Motts had put him at the top of her suspect list.

"Definitely. He never wore any sort of jewellery

that I can remember." Marnie replied. The twins nodded their agreement. "We could ask him."

The evening had been going so well. Motts had handled her crowded living room well. And from one second to the next, she hit the limit of her ability to cope.

Ever the calm and observant one, Nish recognised the signs first. He gathered up the food to store in the fridge. And ignoring the confused mutterings, he ushered River, Marnie and his sister toward the front door.

"Try to relax, Motts. And lock the door behind me." He kissed Cactus on the top of the head before leaving and closing the door behind him.

The peaceful quiet of her cottage went a long way to helping Motts relax. She made sure all the doors and windows had been locked—triple checked the front and back. Cactus followed her faithfully through every room.

"Why am I checking the closet?" Motts peered inside, shifting her coats. "No monsters hiding in the dark."

She tried sleeping in the bedroom. Cactus grumped at her whenever she rolled from one side to the other. *This isn't happening.*

Getting out of bed, Motts wrapped her duvet

around herself. There was no point in trying to pretend to doze. She shuffled into the living room with Cactus riding on the edge of the blanket.

Motts fumbled for the light switch in the hall leading to the open plan living room. She screamed at the face pressed against the glass of the garden window. "What the—"

She froze, as did the man whose face was distorted by the window. He ran while she scrambled to find her phone. It lay on the coffee table next to her laptop.

Her fingers refused to cooperate. Motts eventually managed to dial the police. She sank down on the ground, shivering under the duvet with Cactus prowling around her.

Motts stared at the door. The kind woman on the other end of the phone promised her the knocking came from the police. She was struggling to make herself open it. "I can do this."

"You're going to be fine, love. I promise. Constable Stone is there. Inspector Ash has called in other officers from Looe. They'll find your peeping Tom," she promised. "You can hang up and open the door whenever you're ready."

It took a few seconds to gather her courage. Motts disconnected the call and unlocked the door. Hughie offered her a comforting grin when he came into view.

"No sign of him. And I haven't seen any damage to the door or window. He might've been hunting for something in particular." He stepped inside when Motts moved back. "Are you alright?"

"Fine." Motts didn't know what to say. She was usually the one posing the question because she struggled to decipher facial expressions. "Okay. I wasn't hurt."

"You don't have to be physically attacked to be hurt." Hughie went over to the fire, grabbing a log and stoking the flames. "Let's get things warmed up in here. Can you describe him?"

"Male? Maybe brown hair? It was dark then I flipped the light on, so all I saw were bright spots and a blurry face." Motts kicked herself for not having CCTV cameras installed. She'd never considered needing them in Cornwall. Polperro had always seemed such a safe village. "I wouldn't recognise him if I bumped into him in the street. I'm sorry."

"Don't apologise." Hughie glanced behind him when a knock sounded on the front door. "Want me to check?"

"Please."

He returned with Inspector Ash in tow. "They caught Danny Orchard running down Quay Road. He confessed to being in your garden. Said he was playing a prank."

"How is that a prank?" Motts crossed her arms. She unfolded them and picked up Cactus when he meowed insistently. "Why?"

"Why don't you come ask him? I've got him in my car." Inspector Ash nodded toward the front door. "But only if you feel comfortable. I'm confident I can get answers from him."

"Give me a moment."

Darting back into her bedroom, Motts exchanged her duvet and pyjamas for jeans and a long-sleeved T-shirt. She shoved her feet into slippers. Her hoodie hung on a hook by the front door.

"He's quite secure and can't hurt you," Inspector Ash assured her.

Motts found Danny Orchard more pathetic than intimidating in the back of a police vehicle. He slouched into the seat with the air of a put-upon teenager, not a grown man. "Why were you in my garden?"

He shrugged.

"Did you lock me in the shed?" She didn't doubt he was capable. He was also the most logical suspect.

"What? No. I've got better things to do." Danny seemed genuinely affronted by her question.

"Better than snooping around in the middle of the night and terrifying women?" Inspector Ash cowed the agitated man with a frown. "Your mum won't be best pleased when she finds out. You're too old for this nonsense."

"I thought you found her necklace," Danny shouted. The tears in his eyes made Motts suspect he was genuinely distressed. "My beautiful Rhona. So young and vibrant. Gave her a locket I'd found by the sea. She never took it off. It was delicate like her."

Motts grimaced at the flowery declaration. She found herself questioning whether Danny was the killer. *Would he be so upset if he had done it? Maybe he's a good actor.* "I don't have Rhona's necklace. Inspector Ash has the tin I found. There was no locket inside."

She didn't mention the slender gold chain. He'd worked himself up enough already. His name had definitely moved down her list of suspects to the bottom.

"Her poxy brother abandoned all of her precious belongings at charity shops. I hoped to find her necklace." Danny grew increasingly angry. The words seemed to explode out of him. "Noel never even bothered to tell me until all of it had been sold. How could the bastard toss all her stuff? Like she never existed?

He even took the photos with her off the walls of the fish and chip shop."

Had he? How interesting.

Motts glanced over at Inspector Ash, whose gaze was laser-focused on Danny. She had one last question for the youngest Orchard. "Did you run me over?"

"What? No. Bloody bint."

"Right. That's enough." Inspector Ash slammed the door shut. "Why don't you head inside to get warm? He's not going to tell us anything else."

"Okay." She thanked both the police officers and went inside. Cactus watched her lock the doors for a second time. "Here's hoping the excitement for the day is done."

Thinking back to the conversation, Motts didn't need Danny to say anything else. He'd given her a new name—Noel. And he'd also given her a reason to speak with Innis Walters again. She hoped he'd be more receptive. Maybe if she brought the photos to prod his memory.

She made herself a mug of hot chocolate and sank into the chair by the fire. Cactus leapt up into the seat beside her. "Right. Time to update the mystery."

The primrose mystery.

Motts had saved the images into a file along with a Word document holding her questions. She struck through the ones connected to Danny. "Not one hundred percent certain he's innocent. But I'm also not convinced he could've hurt her."

Meow.

"That's right. I need to know the exact date of Rhona's disappearance and where Danny was." Motts returned to the news article she'd bookmarked. It gave her the date when Rhona had last been seen. "Okay. If Danny helps his family in their gardening business, he can't claim work as an alibi. No one tends plants in the middle of the night."

She hoped Danny would remember his whereabouts. Though, she'd have to wait until the police released him. Inspector Ash wasn't likely to allow her to interrogate the man.

Dozing in her chair, Motts was jolted awake by a pounding on her front door. She glanced at the grandfather clock in the corner. *Ten in the morning. Bugger.* She hadn't intended to sleep in.

"Hang on." Motts stumbled toward the front door, opening it to find Detective Inspector Herceg. "Hello."

"I brought povitica. My mother's version, with dark chocolate." He held up a paper-wrapped package and a carrier with two cups. "And coffee."

"Povitica?"

"A sweet yeast bread with swirls from my native

Croatia. I've tried making them. Mine turns out like a lump of coal every time." He smiled, following her into the cottage. "Ash called me about your adventures. Are you well?"

"Fine."

"Motts."

Motts stared at the detective—at his slightly crooked and strong nose, not his piercing eyes that made it difficult to lie. She didn't feel fine. Her nerves hadn't settled since getting locked in the shed. "You brought coffee."

"Thought you might want some after the long night you had. Mrs Griffin assured me you enjoyed this particular flavour." Teo grabbed one of the cups to set in front of her. "She was quite excited for some reason."

Motts covered her face with her hands and resisted the urge to scream. "Who knows."

Oh, good grief. She'll be on the phone to my auntie Lily to tell her about the new person in my life. And Auntie Lily will call Mum.

And they won't listen to my "he's a nice detective who's trying to solve a case and not date me."

"Are you sure you're okay?"

Motts nodded. *Fine, fine, don't mind my silently screaming into the void.* "So, tell me about povitica."

CHAPTER ELEVEN

"Wherefore art thou, tiny Pineapple?"

"In the garden." Motts smothered her laugh. Her uncle Tom had a flair for the dramatic. And he was one of the few people who occasionally used her proper name. "Did Auntie Lily send you?"

"She did. With food, because everything in life can be solved with a home-cooked meal." He hefted up the large casserole dish in his arms. "One of her unique fusions, her family's special fried rice mixed with a full English breakfast. Tastier than it sounds."

And it was tastier than it sounded. Motts had a great appreciation for her auntie Lily's culinary creations. Crispy sausage, roasted diced potatoes, tomatoes, and scrambled eggs. They went surprisingly well in fried rice.

"A whole casserole for me?"

"I wouldn't say no to a bite. And I know your Cactus will steal sausage with or without your help." He glanced around the yard. "You've made impressive progress. You'll be able to put in your herbs in a month. Are you excited?"

"About herbs?"

Her uncle shook his head with a laugh. "About your little spot of heaven being situated the way you want?"

"I'm happy." Motts got to her feet and dusted off her knees. She'd finally managed to complete sectioning off the garden. It was ready for plants whenever the weather decided to play nice. They'd had a sudden cold snap, but the weatherperson had promised things would warm up in a day or two. "I think."

"You are." He'd always been good about helping her identify emotions, especially at times when her parents struggled. "You were never this relaxed in London."

London had been loud. Full of people, sounds, lights, and smells. The large city had often overwhelmed Motts.

One of the reasons Motts had considered accepting the inherited cottage was the chance to move somewhere quieter. She hadn't expected skeletons to come up out of the ground. Or to become the focus of local gossip and drama. She still enjoyed the calm of the village more than London.

"Here, point me in the direction of the plates, and I'll get lunch sorted." He started toward the cottage while Motts gathered up her gardening tools. "Did River help you get your new scooter sorted?"

"He drove me out to pick it up." Motts deftly dodged Cactus, who'd made his way off his bed by the fireplace to greet her and her uncle. "Patience."

Meow.

"I feel confident that was a 'hurry the hell up.'" Her uncle pried the lid off the casserole dish. He quickly found two plates for them. "Does he need his own bowl?"

Motts glanced at her uncle, trying to decide if he was teasing or being serious. She decided to treat it as a real question. "He'll snack from my plate."

While they ate and her uncle filled her in on the family goings-on, Motts's thoughts drifted to everything that had happened in the last few days. She hadn't delved much into the cold case. Her nerves hadn't fully settled.

During his visit earlier in the week, Detective Inspector Herceg hadn't been too open with divulging information. He thought she shouldn't get drawn further into the case. Motts had dragged a few details out of him.

Danny Orchard had been cleared of any suspicion with regards to the murder, though they'd charged him with trespassing and given him a warning for stalking. He'd been able to provide an ironclad alibi for the night Rhona disappeared. Local rumours about the couple meeting up had simply been gossip.

Gossip or misdirection?

Innis had been quite vocal in his belief that Danny and Rhona had been going out. He'd also had ongoing issues with his sister. Money (and inheritances) tended to bring out the worst in people.

"What are you thinking about, little Pineapple?" Her uncle tapped his fork against her plate. "Not to your liking?"

"It's yummy." She made a concerted effort to focus on the fried rice and her uncle. *Bugger. Don't let your thoughts wander when family is here. They'll think something is wrong.* "Thanks for bringing it."

Why am I so awkward?

"Your dad worries about you."

"Uncle Tomato." Motts didn't want her parents to stress over her being so far away. "I'm doing fine."

"Fine?" he questioned. "We've very different definitions of the word. You'll admit things haven't exactly gone to plan for you thus far."

"No one predicts they're going to find a body buried in a shallow grave in their garden. Do they? I'm managing. It's not the first dead person I've discovered." She thought she'd done remarkably well not to have a complete and total breakdown. "Did you see my garden? I'm doing brilliantly with adulting."

"You are. And I'm proud of you. So are your parents."

"Mum's upset."

"Your mum loves you so much. She's struggling with her only child being so far away." He pointed a rice-covered fork at her. "Don't let her make you nervous. She'll calm down eventually."

Would she? Motts wasn't convinced. Her uncle let the subject go as they finished up their lunch; he didn't press her for anything else.

"Now, don't you go finding any more adventures. Hug?" He opened his arms, waiting for her to decide. She went in for a quick embrace. "And make sure to enjoy the rest of the fried rice for supper. You can bring the casserole dish over on the weekend, if you like."

After seeing her uncle off, Motts grabbed the hollyhock bouquet she'd finished the night before. A client in Yorkshire had ordered it a few weeks ago. She wanted to drop it off at the post office to go in the mail, plus she could stop by the bridal shop to chat with Marnie.

"You're going to be fine." Motts gave herself a pep talk. "No one is going to try to run you over—again."

Breathing in deeply was a definite mistake. Motts pinched the bridge of her nose to stop the sneeze. Flowers all along the cliffs and hedgerows had blossomed as spring took hold.

They were beautiful. Her allergies didn't quite have the same appreciation for them. She'd tried wearing a mask during spring, but they never worked.

Breathing masks made her feel as though she were suffocating. Her mum had tried to force one on her as a child. She'd had the worst meltdown, and the subject had never been broached again.

Visually, though, Polperro had become as beautiful as any painting in a museum. Motts understood why most of her family had never wanted to leave or had returned after a time away. Her mum and dad had been the lone holdouts, preferring life in the bustling city.

It was hard to believe she'd been in Cornwall for two weeks already. Polperro seemed more like home than London ever had to her. And oddly, it made her want to solve the mystery even more.

Motts made the short drive down the hill from her cottage to the post office. She had to smile when Mrs Ferris held the door open for her. "Hello."

"Doc. Come see who's out and about," she yelled into the back while taking the box out of Motts's arms. "We were sick with worry after your crash. It's lovely to see you doing so well. Can I do anything else for you? Need stamps?"

The sweet, adorable couple fussed over Motts. Mrs Ferris reminded her so much of her gran. The older woman even snuck a KitKat into her pocket, something Motts's gran always did when she visited.

On her way out of the post office, Mott's stumbled on a hint of a clue. She spied a photo of four teenagers on the wall by the door. She immediately recognised two of them, Rhona and Danny; she didn't know the others.

"Our grandson, Derek, and two of his best mates. Our boy is away in the military now." Doc joined her. "You'll know Danny Orchard, of course. And his girl, Rhona, the poor dear. God rest her soul. And the last one is Noel Watson. He runs his family's charity shop over on The Coombe."

"Does he?" Motts stood on her tiptoes to get a

closer look at the quartet. Something on Noel's wrist caught her attention. "He's wearing a bracelet."

"His father's. Niall Watson fished with a local fishery. They all got those bracelets one year after a bad storm," Doc commented offhand. He patted her shoulder gently. "You be safe out there, alright?"

Despite wanting to immediately head to the charity shop, Motts didn't want to go on her own. She guided her scooter in the opposite direction to Griffin Brews. It would kill two birds with one stone—coffee and an accomplice.

"Mottsy." Vina almost vaulted the counter to come give her a hug. "Hello, darling. Coffee or tea this fine afternoon?"

"Did they overcharge your personality again?" She patted her ex-girlfriend on the shoulder and extracted herself from the exuberant hug. "Have you or Nish had a lunch break yet?"

"Why?" Nish finished up with a customer. "Tea and biscuits? Coffee? Pastry? Mum outdid herself. She whipped up curry cream and dark chocolate ganache macarons."

"I'll take a shed-load of them." Motts's mouth had already started to water. "And coffee. To go. I'm heading over to the Watson Charity Shop."

"Are you?" Nish paused while placing macarons

into a box. "Vina already had her break. But I can go with you."

"Bastard." Vina flicked him with a rolled-up tea towel. "Here I am doing all the work."

"All the work?" Motts glanced between the twins. "Vina didn't even do all her coursework in university."

"Traitor."

"Are my babies causing problems again?" Leena Griffin came through the swinging door from the kitchen. Her hands and apron were covered in flour. "Did they offer you tea or coffee? Lazy children."

"*Amma,*" Vina complained dramatically.

"Why can't my babies be as sweet and calm as you?" Leena wrapped Motts in a floury and saffron-scented hug. "Are you well?"

"I am the epitome of sweet and calm." Vina went over to help a customer while her brother laughed at her.

"You enjoy the macarons. I've got pasties in the oven." Leena squeezed her one last time, then disappeared into the kitchen.

"So, coffee and treats. And what's this about the charity shop?" Nish handed over the cup and box. "Things have quieted down, so I can go with if you like."

The macarons didn't make it out of the coffee

shop. Motts noshed her way through them rapidly. They had the perfect combination of crunchy outside and soft inside; the sweet and spicy curry cream mingled with the bite of the dark chocolate ganache.

"I could bathe in that." Motts licked the last bit of ganache off her finger. "Does your mum know she's a genius?"

By the time they left the coffee shop, Motts had finished her drink and far too many macarons to be healthy.

They walked the few streets over to the charity shop. Motts stopped a few stores down from Watsons. She didn't usually make impulsive decisions.

"We need a plan."

Nish pulled his attention away from the window display at the jewellers. "This sea glass broach is stunning."

"Nish? A plan?"

"Let's wing it. You'll get stuck trying to remember your conversation script if we plan every nuance of our attempt to weasel information." Nish did have a point. "I'll help."

Her heart started to beat faster the closer they got to the door. Motts tried the breathing exercises River had taught her. They eased the frantic anxiety.

Nish held the door open for her. "After you."

"Has to be, since you're holding the door." She ignored his wry chuckle. "Oh, they have a book section."

"Motts."

Ignoring him, Motts squeezed between racks of clothing to check out the bookshelves running along the right wall. She grabbed a book of poetry by Ann Kelley, a Cornish author. A second one on Cornwall's role in various wars caught her attention; Teo had mentioned an interest in history and battles.

"Are we shopping?" Nish followed her along the aisle.

"Might as well. It's quiet in here." Motts didn't want to spring questions on a complete stranger. "He's likely to be more open to answering if we've bought at least one book."

"Delaying tactics."

"Maybe." Motts grabbed a third book from one of the shelves. "Who's donating graphic novels to a shop in Polperro?"

Instead of answering, Nish held his arms out. She piled up a few including *The Encyclopaedia of Early Earth*, one she'd been wanting to read for a few years. *The Wicked + The Divine* also made it onto the stack.

"My arms are going to snap." Nish leaned his head

around the books when Motts went to add yet another one. "Can you even fit all these on your scooter?"

"Good point." She reluctantly put back one of the Mouse Guard series by David Peterson. "I'll come back for these."

"Are you ready for the questioning phase of this adventure?" Nish cautiously manoeuvred through the cramped shop in the general direction of the till. "A little help?"

Motts grabbed his arm to stop him from careening into a table of posh perfumes. "Sorry. Here, I'll guide you."

"Hello there."

Motts recognised the pleasant man who greeted them from behind the till. He hadn't changed much from the photo of him during his younger days. "You're Noel."

"I am." He smiled, taking the books to calculate the cost. "Did you find everything you needed? We've a fair few books at the mo'."

"I saw a photo of you at the post office." Motts tried for casual; from Nish's quiet laugh, she hadn't quite succeeded. "You knew Rhona."

Noel's friendly grin disappeared in an instant. "Three quid for the lot of books."

Motts exchanged a glance with Nish, who shook

his head subtly. She fished out a fiver and handed it over. "Did you know her well?"

"Mind your own business." He slammed her change on the counter and fled into the back room of the shop.

"Well, that's us told." Nish gathered up her books. "Come on, I'll carry these back over to the café for you."

Why is everyone so testy when it comes to even mentioning Rhona's name?

CHAPTER TWELVE

"I can do without your help." Motts gently lifted the paw from the page. Cactus loved to nudge at her book while she read. "Meowing at me won't change my mind."

She'd hung out at Griffin Brews in the kitchen for a while, helping Vina and her mum make dough. They sent her home with more macarons and a few lamb biryani pasties. It made the perfect combination for an early supper.

Curling up in her new favourite armchair, mostly because of its proximity to the warmth of the fire, Motts had one of her newly acquired graphic novels, a mug of tea, and the box of yummy biscuits. Cactus had tried to steal the macarons several times. She'd managed to keep them out of his little paws.

He didn't seem to understand chocolate wasn't for kitties. She'd obviously spoilt him rotten. Her sweet little naked baby. She covered him more securely with the edge of the blanket.

Motts closed her book and bent forward to place it on the coffee table. She'd struggled to focus all evening. Her mind kept going to their brief encounter with Noel.

Why had he shut down so instantly at the mention of Rhona's name? It made no sense. Motts hadn't asked any probing questions.

The men in Rhona's life all seemed intensely sensitive to even the mention of her name. Instead of clearing them, it made them even more suspect. She wondered if Teo was aware of Noel.

I could send him an email.

Plymouth isn't that far away—maybe too far for a scooter ride.

Or, I can send him a message and spare myself the agonising anxiety and stress.

In theory, email was less stressful than an impromptu in-person visit. In actuality, Motts dithered for thirty minutes over the wording of the subject line. She managed after an hour and a half to get through the message.

Hit send.

Hit send.

Hit send.

Oh my god, I hit send.

Motts closed her laptop, left it on the coffee table, and hid behind the sofa for a few minutes. "Oh, honestly, why am I the way that I am? Overdramatic much?"

No matter how much Motts berated herself, every aspect of sending and receiving messages, whether text or email, caused her stress. She'd tried a myriad of methods to control the anxiety; none of them actually helped.

Just looking at her laptop caused her heart rate to spike up rapidly. Motts breathed in and out slowly until her pulse settled. She stared at her computer for a second more.

"I won't know if Teo responded unless I look, will I?" Motts forced herself to stand up. "Never has my computer appeared more terrifying."

Teo had not responded. Her inbox contained a fifteen-paragraph update from her dad. He told her all about the squirrels showing up in their garden; he was in the midst of a battle trying to keep the little critters from eating the birdseed.

A second email from her cousin about the dinner invite to his parents' place warned her about Auntie

Lily wanting to set her up on a blind date. *I guess I'll be coming down with a sudden case of plague. That sounds plausible. Can't eat with you, I'm going to die.*

Die of embarrassment.

After sending a panicked response to River, Motts found a new message. Teo politely reminded her not to get too close to the investigation. He worried.

Why does his worrying make me feel happy?

Weird, but happy?

The detective hadn't known about the connection with Noel. Teo agreed the intense reaction to Rhona's name was at the very least odd. He didn't say whether he planned to follow up.

The message was a satisfyingly unsatisfying email. Motts's curiosity had only increased with the lack of knowledge. *Is he going to talk to Noel? Or maybe to Doc Ferris? Perhaps I should stop by the post office again.*

Or ask Marnie.

In the excitement of her charity shop finds, Motts had forgotten to visit Marnie. She'd go by after breakfast in the morning. *Here's hoping I manage to stay out of trouble in the process.*

As the evening progressed, Motts found herself dreading bedtime. She kept finding chores to finish. Dishes, dusting, folding laundry, cleaning out Moss's terrarium, reorganising her books in a variety of different ways. It was three in the morning when her exhaustion caught up to her.

She crawled into bed on top of the covers and stared anxiously out the bedroom window into the darkness. Cactus leapt upon the duvet beside her. "What if he's out there again?"

Her mind played tricks on her. Every little sound had her convinced a break-in was imminent. She sat up, scooting up against the headboard with pillows and her multiple blankets making a buffer zone around her body.

Despite her attempts to doze, Motts kept opening her eyes to watch the window. She found the anticipation of something happening almost worse than the actuality of it. Cactus clambered over to flop in her lap, offering a warm and purring sort of comfort.

Motts grabbed her mobile from the nightstand. Her fingers trembled, and she tightened them around the phone. *You can ask for help. Everyone says so.*

They never mention how hard it's going to be, though.

After another ten minutes of not sleeping, Motts scrolled through her contacts. She messaged Vina, the person most likely to be awake. Also the one who'd never get angry at being disturbed.

She hated bothering people. It made phone calls almost impossible. She tended to get eaten up with anxiety over it.

Vina arrived ten minutes later with a coat covering her pyjamas. She had a large thermos in one hand and a bag in the other. "I brought Amma's warm milk tea and spiced scones."

"Your mum was awake?"

"Not sure she ever sleeps." Vina shrugged. "But she was sleeping, don't worry. We made these in the coffee shop, so I popped by to steal a few."

"Is it stealing if you own the café?" Motts crossed her legs and had to smile when Cactus curled up between them. "I shouldn't be so scared. I'm fine. They caught Danny. He's not going to peer in my windows again."

"Fear is fear, Mottsy." Vina bent forward to gently squeeze her knee. "Glad you called. I was dealing with a bout of insomnia myself."

"Why?"

"I met someone." She quickly shoved half a scone into her mouth.

"Did you?" Motts took a sip of tea, sighing contentedly at the familiar flavour. She had no idea how Leena made it so delicious. "And? Are you happy?"

Vina shrugged. "Do you ever regret our breakup?"

Motts hesitated for a minute. She never knew if non-autistics wanted honest answers to difficult questions. "I...."

"Truthfully," Vina prompted.

"Not really." Motts kept her gaze on her mug of tea. "You know you're my best friend. You, Nish, and River. You've all been my only friends. We didn't work as a couple."

"We could've."

"You wanted sex. I'm not into sex," Motts said matter-of-factly. "Do you regret it?"

"No." Vina licked the sticky glaze from the scone off her fingers. "I'd have missed you if we hadn't stayed friends. That mattered more to me."

"Good. We've answered a pointless question to distract from your bombshell. Tell me about your new girlfriend." Motts poked Vina on the bottom of her sock-covered foot. "Are there pictures? Have you told your family?"

"You're the first in the family I've told."

Motts gave her a watery smile. She was moved to know Vina considered her family. "Well? What's her name? Is she local?"

"Taara. Taara Khatri. She's Punjabi. Travels between Lahore and London for her family's company. They import herbs and spices for Indian restaurants and shops across England." Vina twisted her phone around to show Motts a photo. "She's so out of my league."

"How?" Motts studied the image of the stylish woman. "She dresses better."

"Rude."

"You live in jeans and long-sleeved hoodies." Motts glanced down at her own pyjamas. "Granted, I once spent an entire month wearing the same soft penguin onesie. So, who am I to judge?"

"She's gorgeous."

"She's very aesthetically pleasing." Motts thought both Vina and her new girlfriend were equally stunning. She didn't see the point in comparison. "And so are you."

"We've got to work on your compliment skills." Vina reached into the bag she'd brought and pulled out a packet of Jaffa Cakes. "Found these tucked in the cupboard at home. Pretty sure Nish hid them for you."

Munching on the biscuits, Motts tried to sort out her feelings. She was pleased for Vina. Her friend deserved every ounce of happiness in the world.

And Motts meant what she'd said earlier. Their relationship, as a romantic one, had been doomed for failure. They hadn't been sexually compatible.

Their friendship had mattered more.

Motts snagged a second Jaffa Cake. "I'm happy for you."

Vina considered her for a moment before breaking into a smile. "Brilliant. I'm so relieved. Now I just have to introduce her to the family. You'll be there, right? I need moral support. Amma compares every date I have to you."

"Weird."

"Not really. You're the only person who doesn't seem to grasp what a magnificent person you are." Vina pointed the mug at her. "See. There you go. Shrinking into yourself like Moss, pulling her head into her shell. You do know compliments are good things, right?"

Motts shrugged.

"Do you want to talk about your anxiety attack?" Vina moved the conversation to another topic; Motts didn't find this one any easier than compliments. "Was it the peeping Tom episode?"

"Am I ever going to feel safe in the cottage?" Motts grabbed Cactus, hugging him to her chest. "I keep seeing faces in the shadows in the dark."

"Of course you will." Her friend shifted up to sit next to her, wrapping an arm around Motts. "It's going to take time."

"How much?"

"I don't know."

Two days later, Motts was exhausted from struggling with fear-induced insomnia. She had managed to unpack, clean, and organise every inch of her cottage. The garden looked immaculate. She'd gotten some of her new herbs and plants into the ground.

Sleep?

Sleep had been one thing she hadn't managed successfully. She'd been catnapping, which wasn't as healthy for her as it was Cactus. Nothing seemed to help, not even the herbal tea Auntie Lily sent over with River.

Motts had moved from her backyard to the front of the cottage. There were boxes under the two front windows and a tiny plot to the left of the door. She'd dug up all the flowers and handed them off to her uncle Tom for his garden.

The sound of a car driving up the lane towards her cottage caught her attention. Motts glanced up to find Detective Inspector Herceg climbing out of his vehicle. He waved, moving around to the boot and retrieving a large box.

Motts sat back on her heels with her trowel in

hand. "Has something happened? Did you have a break in the case?"

A break in the case?

I've been watching way too much Rosemary & Thyme.

And Father Brown.

And every other mystery show available on the internet.

"Can't speak on the case." He carried the box over and balanced it against his side. "I'll say we're following up on a few leads."

"Police always say that on the telly when they don't have any leads at all." Motts had been taking notes from how they handled investigations in shows. "What's in the box?"

"Shows aren't always based completely in fact." Detective Herceg tilted the box slightly to reveal the contents. "Motion-activated outdoor lights for the front and back of your cottage. I also have a CCTV system for you, along with one of those doorbells with a webcam. You can download apps to your tablet or phone. You never have to wonder who's out in the dark. The lights will let you know, and the cameras will provide another layer of protection."

Motts got to her feet and brushed nervously at the dirt on her jeans. "I don't know what to say."

He hefted the box in his arm. "Don't need to say anything aside from giving me permission to install it. I won't if you aren't interested."

"But why?" Motts crossed her arms, huffing in annoyance when dirt from the trowel got on her shirt. "Is this a service detective inspectors provide to the community?"

"Not quite." He patted the box with one hand. "I wanted you to feel safe in your cottage. And this technology might help."

Motts didn't know how to respond. She decided maybe they should head inside to finish the conversation. "Would you like tea?"

"If you don't mind, we can talk over the details." He followed her into the cottage and placed the box on the small table in the kitchen. "The cameras and lights are ones I'm familiar with. I used them on my place and my parents'."

"Thank you."

"Thank me by getting some sleep, yeah?" Teo began lifting items out of the box. He had four lights to cover the entire property. "You're safe here."

Motts watched him get to work installing the cameras. "I'll do my best."

CHAPTER THIRTEEN

With the lights and cameras, Motts managed to sleep well for the first time in days. She discovered that once again village gossip had been the culprit in ratting her out to Teo. Nish had mentioned it to Hughie, who'd told Inspector Ash, who'd casually shared the information with Detective Inspector Herceg.

Wonderful.

She wasn't entirely sure how to feel about the rumour vine. Unlike her bad experiences in school, this one seemed determined to make her life better. She decided not to worry about it.

Why worry about it? Her dad had always told her not to worry about other people. She could only control herself.

She had other things to worry about.

Who had killed Rhona Walters? The question haunted her almost as much as the ones she had about Jenny's death. Two young women taken under disturbing circumstances.

With her insomnia dealt with, Motts had a new drive to solve the mystery. She'd decided to confront Danny directly. First about why he'd been at her place, and second about the day Rhona disappeared.

March had brought them beautifully sunny weather. Motts took advantage of it by getting out her bicycle. She rode down the hill from the cottage and made her way to the nursery the Orchards ran as part of their gardening business.

"What do you want?" Danny Orchard Sr. blocked the entrance to the nursery. He had a shovel in one hand and rested his arms against the top. "Haven't you caused us enough trouble?"

"Me?" Motts considered getting back on her bicycle and racing away. She wanted answers, though. "I haven't done anything. Your son decided to trespass on my property in the middle of the night. And I'd like to ask him a few questions about why."

"You're—"

"Let me handle this." Danny stepped around his father, shoving him into the shop and closing the door on him. "Sorry. He can be a right bastard when he wants."

Motts stared at Danny, unsure of how to proceed. "Why?" she began and stopped, still not confident what to actually ask.

Why?

Why brain?

How is "why" going to help?

"Why did you scare me half to death?" Motts decided to try for a second time with a complete sentence.

Danny rubbed his hand along the back of his neck. He motioned for her to follow him down the sidewalk, away from the front of the nursery. "After Rhona's body was found, I'd heard you discovered clues. I wanted to see if you'd figured out who killed her."

"Why?"

"I *loved* her," Danny practically shouted at her. He held his hands up when she started to back away. "Sorry, I'm sorry. Rhona was my everything. We'd dated without anyone knowing for ages. Innis didn't approve of me. We were going to elope. Eventually."

"Okay. Did you know about the box hidden in my garden?" Motts showed him the images from her phone. "Was the bracelet yours?"

"The necklace and earring were Rhona's. I bought

them for her. No idea who took the photo. A few blokes in the village used to have that bracelet. Our own little club." Danny scratched his jaw and finally handed the phone back to her. "I had no idea who stole the jewellery or buried it."

Motts wasn't sure she believed him but continued with a different question. "Were you meeting her that night?"

Danny shook his head quickly. "She was having a girls' night. One of her friends had messaged her to go out."

"To London?"

"No, don't be daft. Who'd drive up to London for a night?" Danny retorted. "Who said that?"

"Innis."

"Of course, he did. He hated Rhona. Bastard." Danny leaned closer to her. "I always thought he'd done it."

"Oh?" Motts moved Danny from suspect to potentially helpful witness in her mind. "He's grumpy as all get out, but not every cranky human commits murder."

"Innis wanted complete ownership of the Salty Seaman. Rhona had 51 percent. They never told anyone. Her brother wanted to run the place while she wanted out of Cornwall." He stopped when they reached the corner. "She let him manage the shop, never once questioned him on what he did."

"Then why would he care about her having 51 percent?"

"She wanted to sell the place."

"Oh." Motts had no doubts Innis would've fought tooth and nail to keep the Salty Seaman in the family. "Was there a buyer?"

"She never said." Danny glanced behind them when someone shouted his name. "They'll be wanting me for a delivery. I am sorry for scaring you the other night. It was a dreadful thing to do. My mum read me the riot act when I got home from the police station."

Motts bit back her instinctual response of "it's okay," because it wasn't. "Try not to do it again, alright?"

"Right." Danny nodded, then jogged down the sidewalk.

Walking her bike a little further, Motts considered the brief conversation. Danny had dumped a load of information on her. She wondered if the police had pulled Rhona's text messages. Did mobile companies keep the records on those for years? Or delete them?

She rode into the central part of the village. The Salty Seaman caught her attention down the street.

She had another hour or so before they opened for lunch.

The bridal shop opened much earlier in the day, as did Griffin Brews. Motts decided to swing by Marnie's to see what she thought about her conversation with Danny. And then she'd visit Vina and Nish.

"Hello, Mottley crew." Marnie waved her inside. "You've impeccable timing. I've got an order for you."

Motts had decided not to stress over the random nicknames Marnie tossed her way on occasion. "I had a chat with Danny."

"You didn't."

"I did."

"You didn't." Marnie covered her face with her hands, shaking her head with a laugh. "My Perry will lose his mind if he finds out. Why on earth would you talk to that reprobate?"

"I can't ignore him. We live in the same village. A small village. And their gardening business is right at the end of my street." Motts left out the part where she hadn't actually stopped investigating. "Am I supposed to run across the street screaming if I see him?"

"And you wanted to know about him and Rhona?" Marnie said knowingly. "Here. Sit with me behind the counter. I'm finishing up this lace veil, and you can tell me about your gossipy chat with Danny."

"Are you psychic?"

Marnie threw her head back and laughed loudly. "I know people. You'll be surprised how much you can learn helping brides. All the families coming in with them. The worst and the best in people happen while they're trying on their dresses."

What did that even mean? Motts tried not to worry about it and carried on. She told Marnie all about her chat with Danny.

"Fifty-one percent?" Marnie interrupted her mid-retelling. "He said that specific number? Rose always said the siblings had equal control."

"Apparently not." Motts played with the zipper on the light jacket she'd worn. "And Danny swears he had nothing to do with her murder. He claims they were going to elope."

"Innis would've hunted them both down."

"Why?"

"The family was pretty old-fashioned. Innis took after his father. Rhona, for all her sweetness, was a bit of a rebel." Marnie set the veil aside. She bent down to find an album on one of the cabinets along the wall. "I always snap a photo of the bridal parties. Here's one from Innis and Rose's wedding."

Motts glanced at the photo. "Rhona definitely doesn't seem part of the group."

In the photo of women, Rhona was slouched off to the side, a physical separation between her and the rest of the bridal party. Her eyes were focused away from the camera.

"Sulked the entire day." Marnie leaned down to see the photo better. "Rose had included her for Innis's sake. As sweet as Rose can be, I don't think the two women got along overly well. Rhona went through a difficult phase after their parents passed away. She wanted so hard to move away from our little village. She felt trapped by the weight of family history."

"Danny claimed she'd wanted to sell the Salty Seaman." She handed the album back to Marnie. "I'm guessing Innis wouldn't have agreed."

"If she had controlling interest, he wouldn't have been able to stop her." Marnie clucked her tongue and shook her head. "He'd have been furious with his sister. He lives and breathes the restaurant."

"The plot thickens."

Was the potential sale of a family business impetus for murder? Motts had heard over and over on true crime shows how money tended to be one of the strongest motivators. She wondered if Teo would want to know what she'd discovered.

Granted, he probably already knew. Motts thought

he was an incredibly thorough investigator. He wouldn't leave any stone unturned to solve the case.

It wouldn't hurt to message him.

"You know," Marnie interrupted her thoughts, "I didn't bring my packed lunch."

"Oh?"

"I'm craving something salty and greasy." She winked at Motts. "What about you? Fancy fish and chips? Maybe a dash of vinegar. There's a brilliant place just down the road. Maybe you've heard of it?"

Teasing.

She's joking.

Motts took a moment to realise Marnie was having a laugh with her. She forced herself to grin, though, as always, a little delayed. "Are they open?"

Marnie glanced at the delicate watch on her wrist. "Should be. First chips are always the best chips."

"Why?"

Flipping the sign on her shop, Marnie held the door open for Motts. She didn't seem to have an answer for Motts. They debated the best time to get chips all the way down the street.

She still wasn't completely sold on the idea of early chips being the greatest. How did the time of day matter? It was one of those questions that would roll around in her mind for days. She had a habit of getting hyperfocused on things she didn't understand.

"What are you doing?" Marnie asked when Motts stopped and pulled out her phone.

"Texting myself to buy chips when a shop opens, in the middle of the day, and right before it closes. A scientific experiment to determine if early is actually best." Motts finished the message, hit send, and slipped her phone back into her pocket. She shifted uncomfortably as Marnie blinked in surprise at her. "I like being thorough."

Also, I'm autistic and unable to allow questions like these to sit without seeing if I can answer them.

Being diagnosed later in life, Motts sometimes felt like saying "I'm autistic" might be construed as an excuse. Nish had told her in the past that not everyone needed or deserved to know. It was her story—not anyone else's.

He'd also explained to her about how imposter syndrome might make her feel as though some of her experience wasn't real. "That's bullshit, Motts," he'd said. "Sometimes, you have to ignore the jerk in your head. Just because everyone doesn't experience it, doesn't mean you're not going through something."

Nish, above almost everyone else around her, had helped Motts learn to breathe again, shedding the skin of her life before understanding why her brain behaved the way it did. It had been a moment of freedom but also terror.

She had spent months and even years learning how to be her true self—not the version developed over years of trying to be non-autistic. Nish had come to see her and helped her. He'd shared his own experiences of finding the courage to be himself. His joy and relief of settling into his skin when society had wanted to force him into a label.

"Shall we?" Marnie drew her out of her memories. She nodded toward the door of the fish and chip shop. "Chin up. Let's see if we can't weasel out some information."

"Isn't your husband going to be upset?"

"What Inspector Perry Ash doesn't know can't hurt me." She grinned. "Besides, we're picking up lunch. Nothing suspicious at all."

"How many times were you suspended from school?" Motts couldn't help the question.

"Me? I was a perfect angel." Marnie grabbed the door and eased it open. "Only once; I locked the school bully in a supply closet, then refused to apologise."

"I like your style." Motts followed her into the chip shop. She remembered to breathe calmly when a glowering Innis stared at them from over the counter. "Hello."

"Quit your frowning." Marnie stepped up next to her. "We're here for lunch. Are you serving or about to berate us for daring to bother you?"

"Innis." Rose slipped by her husband. She had a basket of chips for the fryer. "Don't mind grumpy guts. He wakes up on the wrong side of the world every morning."

After placing their order, they hung out by the counter, chatting with Rose. Motts was greatly impressed by Marnie's ability to ease everyone into small talk. She had the couple nattering away about business within minutes.

When Innis disappeared into the back, Marnie bent forward to Rose. She couched the question about Rhona's wanting to sell gently. But Motts still didn't expect an answer.

To her surprise, Rose blurted out the full truth. Rhona had wanted to sell. The siblings had fallen out over the matter.

Despite the controlling interest, their father's will had stipulated both Rhona and Innis had to agree before the business could be sold. Rose had apparently hoped to convince the two to reconcile. She'd convinced her husband to buy out Rhona's side, an obvious compromise.

Rhona had declined.

Why?

If she wanted to sell, why decline?

It didn't make sense. Motts would think if Rhona wanted to sell to get rid of the shop, she wouldn't have argued with the perfect solution.

There's definitely more to this story.

Innis returned, shutting down the conversation, and practically strong-arming them out of the shop. "Quit asking questions about my family. It's none of your damn business."

CHAPTER FOURTEEN

By the end of the day, Motts discovered Marnie hadn't managed to keep the secret. She was stirring up hot chocolate on the stove when someone knocked on the door. The app on her phone told her Detective Inspector Herceg stood waiting for her.

"You poked the bear."

"I haven't poked any bears. I have all of my fingers." Motts wriggled said digits at him. She welcomed him into the house. "Want some hot chocolate? My dad's recipe. It's a magical potion worthy of Harry Potter."

"How can I say no?" He followed her down the hall into the kitchen, sitting in one of the chairs by the table and making it creak. "Why don't you tell me about your adventures yesterday? The ones not involving poking any bears—even Innis Walters-shaped ones."

Motts poured hot chocolate into two mugs and set one in front of Teo. She sat across from him, stirring the spoon around nervously. "You might be bored."

"I doubt it."

She smiled down at her mug. "I ran into Danny."

"On purpose?"

"I didn't run him over." Motts went on to explain her brief conversation with Danny. Teo seemed particularly interested in his mentioning of Rhona and Innis's contentious relationship. "And I don't believe he killed her."

"Oh?" He bent forward with his elbows on the table. "Aside from his alibi?"

Motts found it easier to stare at her mug than to meet Teo's intense gaze. "Even without the alibi, Danny might be an impulsive, window-peeping prat. He wouldn't have killed her. His devastation at her death seemed too tangibly real. Tangible tangent trembling."

"Not the best alliteration I've heard from you." Teo grabbed the notebook from his jacket pocket. "Did Danny have anything else to say?"

"Other than that?" She hesitated. "I went by a charity shop and spoke to Noel Watson. He had an intense overreaction to my mentioning Rhona's name."

"Did he?"

"And he owned a bracelet similar to the one found in the chest in my garden." Motts glanced up when his pen stopped moving. "I didn't intend to investigate. It's just—unanswered questions bother me so much. I had to know if the bracelet was his."

"He shouted at you." Teo fixated on one part of her story. "Because you asked if he knew Rhona? Someone who'd lived local, gone to school with him, and he'd obviously have known even if just by name."

"Yes."

"And he shouted at you?"

"I said yes." Motts didn't know why he kept repeating it. She decided to brush it off as a weird non-autistic thing. "Did they figure out how she died?"

He closed his notebook and rested his pen on top. "I can't give you any details. I will say they found no evidence of physical trauma."

No evidence of physical trauma.

What did he mean?

Had Rhona died from suffocation or poison or something that hadn't damaged her bones?

"Did they test the flowers in the chest?"

"Foxglove."

Motts sat up quickly, and her arm almost knocked over the hot chocolate. "Foxglove? Isn't it poisonous?"

"Motts." Teo had resumed his serious detective inspector frowning persona. He finished up his hot chocolate and got to his feet. "I'll see myself out. Please don't go pressing for more answers. We don't know who tried to run you over. I don't want them focusing their attention on you again. Okay?"

Motts nodded absently. She grabbed both mugs and set them in the sink, filling them with water. "Did you stop by for any reason?"

"Oh, yes. Inspector Ash told me you'd paid a visit to the Salty Seaman. I wanted to make sure you were alright." He rested a hand on her shoulder, squeezing gently before heading towards the front door. "Lock up behind me."

And she did.

Meow.

Motts finished pushing the deadlock across, then picked up Cactus. "Why don't we have a little snack? Would you like chicken or some cheese?"

Meow.

"Cheese it is. I'll have crackers." Motts grabbed a packet of Jacob's, buttered a handful, and sliced up some aged cheddar. "Why don't we see what's on YouTube?"

Catching up on her many subscriptions, Motts fed Cactus a few slivers of cheese. They munched on their snacks. She couldn't stop thinking about Innis and Noel.

To her, they were the strongest suspects with Danny proving himself innocent. She put Innis above Noel. The latter didn't seem to have any motive whatsoever.

Did he give her a strange vibe? Yes. Was it enough to accuse him of murder? No.

"What a strange place I've moved us to." Motts cuddled Cactus into her arms, shoving the plate across the table. "Do you think Auntie Daisy had any idea? Probably not."

Meow.

"Yes, I am going to have a bath." Motts placed Cactus on the sofa. She dropped a few veggies in for Moss, making sure all was well in the turtle's world. "The more I live here, the more I realise what a small world London had become for me."

Running the water for a bath, Motts grabbed her laptop. She set it up on the sink at an angle to allow her to watch one of her video playlists. And after checking all the windows and doors, she returned to the bathroom and dropped a bath bomb into the water and watched the fizzing.

Motts had one foot in the water when the sound of glass breaking caused her to freeze. "What the—"

She shoved her clothes back on. Cactus sat in the hallway, hissing viciously. She dialled the police while inching her way forward.

"I have a weapon," Motts lied. She grabbed the broom leaning against the wall and rounded the corner to find nothing but a broken front window and a large rock on the carpet. "Bugger. Why me?"

It didn't surprise her when Teo and Inspector Ash showed up with Hughie. The three men were more serious than she'd ever seen them. She watched from inside while they inspected the outside.

"I'm going to need you to download your CCTV footage for me. You likely caught the crime on camera." Inspector Ash wandered over to speak with Hughie.

"Can't I leave you alone for a second?" Teo loomed over her. He seemed so much taller all of a sudden. "Did you see anyone?"

"No." Motts was annoyed to find herself blushing at the thought of mentioning she'd been in the bath. *What kind of nonsense is this? It's a bath—everyone bathes, Motts.* "I wasn't in the living room at the time. I was getting in the bath."

"Were you?" He cleared his throat, turned around, and went over to Perry Ash.

Men (and neurotypicals especially) can be so strange.

"Are you alright?" Hughie came over to sit beside her on the bench in front of the cottage. "I've called a bloke I know. He'll be over in a jiffy to fix your window. Doesn't even need to measure, since he fit the windows for your auntie a few years ago."

"Okay." Motts wrapped her arms around herself. She rocked slightly on the bench, trying to ease some of the tension in her body. Now was not the time to have a meltdown or a shutdown. "Okay. Okay. Broken bashed battered babbling boomer."

"You sure you're alright?" Hughie asked. "Do you need to visit the doctor?"

She shook her head rapidly. "I'm fine."

"Stone. Over here." Inspector Ash interrupted their awkward attempt at small talk. "We've got the video from the security cameras. Take a look."

While the two locals viewed the footage from her CCTV camera, Teo came over and sat beside her. He reached into his pocket to retrieve a package. Motts blinked when a chocolate bar appeared in his hand.

"Lemon Meringue White Chocolate." Her mouth

watered thinking about the combination. "Kernow Chocolate. They're wizards."

"Probably use cauldrons and potions to keep us addicted. Might need to investigate further."

"By purchasing and taste testing more flavours?" Motts peeled back the wrapper of the chocolate. She broke off a few bars and offered it to Teo. "I'd recommend thorough research. Might have to try multiple times to get a complete assessment."

"Agreed." He popped the chocolate into his mouth. "Is your attack kitten safe? And your turtle-tank?"

"Moss is not a tank. She lives in one." Motts stared down at the remaining chocolate in her hand. "I put Cactus in my room until I clean the glass up."

They sat in silence for a while. Teo went over to the other two police officers to check out the video. Motts watched them from the bench. So much for her plans for a relaxing evening.

True to his word, Hughie's friend showed up and immediately got to work with one of his employees to take out the broken window and replace it. Motts used her gardening gloves to pick up the larger pieces, then swept the rest before vacuuming, just to be sure. She'd never forgive herself if Cactus got a sliver in his paw.

Hughie and Teo carried out the glass. They also

checked her garden and made certain the cameras and lights were functioning correctly. It was almost midnight by the time Motts had the house to herself.

They hadn't told her what they found on the CCTV footage. Motts decided to take a look for herself. She went to grab her laptop, only to change directions when someone knocked on the door.

She checked the app on her phone and found Nish, River, and Vina making faces into the camera. *I love my family.* They crowded into the cottage when she opened the door, carrying her along with them into the living room. "You're all out late."

"Marnie texted me after her hubby got home," Vina explained. "I messaged River and Nish, who were out with friends in Looe. They picked up a takeaway and then me. And here we are. We've got pizza, chips, and apparently deep-fried something from the smell."

"Mars bars. You'll thank me later." River grabbed the massive paper sack from Nish. "Someone get plates. I got a few bottles of ale as well."

"So, basically, you brought me a heart attack." Motts accepted the bottle Nish held out to her. She narrowed her eyes on her cousin. "Did you two have a date?"

"We went to a small concert with a group of friends," River insisted. "Vina? Where are the plates?"

"They were on a date." Vina came over from the kitchen with four plates and an assortment of silverware. "Isn't it adorable? We'll be related and everything."

"One date. Vina. One." Nish flicked his sister on the arm. "Let's not have wedding bells ringing."

Seeing how uncomfortable River was getting, Motts decided to provide a distraction. She explained to everyone what had happened with her window. They were as anxious as she was to see the video footage.

They plated up the food, divvying out pizza and chips. The fried candy bars would be left for last. Motts planned to leave those for everyone else; she didn't want to ruin her chocolate palate with bizarre, greasy sweetness.

"Here we go." Motts had her laptop on the end of the coffee table. They'd all sat on the floor around it to eat. She hit play on the video clip from when the rock was thrown; she rewound it a few times before finally pausing it on the person. "That's not—"

"A bloke," River finished for her.

The video clearly showed a slight figure with

generous curves. She had a hoodie on, shielding her face. The woman had a rock already in hand and launched it directly at the front window before fleeing on foot.

"A woman." Vina eased the laptop closer. "I can't see any identifying features. It could be any number of people in the village."

"Could be you," Nish teased.

"I don't do anything that requires me to run." She grabbed her brother's pizza to take a bite. "The important question is, how are we going to hunt this person down?"

"Ten to one, this ends badly," Nish remarked when River jumped on board with the idea.

"We're not hunting anyone down." Motts grabbed another slice of pizza, fending off Cactus's attempt to steal a piece of pepperoni. "The police can handle things."

All three of them turned to stare at her. Motts blocked their gazes with her plate. She conveniently chose not to think about the questions she'd been asking around the village.

Questions weren't the same as going after someone with pitchforks. The trio bantered back and forth. Motts ignored them and finished her pizza slice.

Meow.

Motts glanced over at Cactus, who'd climbed up to

perch on her shoulder. "I agree. I think they need to sleep."

They finished up their incredibly late supper. Vina insisted on watching the CCTV video several more times. She was convinced the way the mysterious figure walked was familiar.

"Doesn't seem different from anyone else's walk." Motts didn't really see what she was talking about.

"You don't watch women's arses when they walk." Vina offered a tiny piece of crust to Cactus, who knocked it to the floor and proceeded to play with the bit of pizza. "I've seen this woman in the village."

"So, what are we going to do? Sit outside the café and observe people for days on end?" Nish grabbed the last chip in the packet. "We do have jobs."

"We'll figure it out." Vina patted Motts on the hand. "No one is going to mess with our Mottsy."

The following morning, Motts woke to find her bed crowded by her cousin and the twins. Cactus had curled up on top of Vina's head. She snuck out of the room to keep her routine.

She brushed her teeth, splashed water on her face, and walked Cactus around her little garden. "What are we going to do? I'm not running away. I love this cottage even though we haven't been here long. I can see making this home forever."

Meow.

"Exactly. It's sized perfectly for us. I'm even growing catnip for you. We'll have to make sure you don't become addicted." Motts crouched down to check on some of the new plants. They wouldn't bud for a while. She continued to obsessively monitor them anyway. "We better head inside and start breakfast."

Meow.

"No, you can't eat an entire package of bacon or sausage. You're going to have to share." Motts led her cat inside. She set him up on the blankets by the rear window. He enjoyed watching the birds who took advantage of the feeders and bath in the garden. "Live-action telly for you."

Moving into the kitchen, Motts grabbed eggs, bacon, and some freshly baked bread. She knew the others would wake up starving. River definitely would.

She dropped bread into the toaster but didn't push it down yet. "I can hear you hovering."

"Can I help?" Vina had Motts's bathrobe wrapped around her. "Heard the detective brought you chocolate."

"He did." Motts focused her attention on cracking eggs into a bowl. She dropped the shells into a little bucket under the sink. "Kernow."

"Your favourite." Vina nudged her gently with her elbow. "He's *aesthetically* pleasing."

"Don't tease." Motts didn't have the energy to deal with joking. She felt like an overly wrung out tea towel. "I'm not up for it."

"Sorry." She wrapped an arm around Motts and hugged her. "I'm sorry your move to the seaside has been marred by all this nonsense. We'll get it solved."

"The police will." Motts whisked up the eggs. She added a dash of seasoning, her own blend. She couldn't wait for her garden to grow to have fresh herbs again. "I trust them."

"You trust him," Vina corrected. She grabbed the packet of bacon. "Bacon or sausage? Or, both?"

"Both. The boys will be hungry." Motts genuinely hoped her cousin and one of her closest friends did develop a romantic relationship. They'd be perfect together. "Get the kettle going? I'm going to need buckets of coffee to wake up."

"I slept great."

"You can sleep anywhere. You could sleep on top of a moving train." Motts hadn't been able to settle down with her overcrowded bed. She'd mostly dozed until about six in the morning. "There was a bed in the spare room."

"You clearly don't grasp the importance of sleepovers."

"Think we're too old for sleepovers. My body definitely is. I find new aches and pains every morning," Motts grumbled. "And hot flashes. I'm dying of heat even when it's snowing outside."

"Age comes for us all."

"Age came for me early. Nothing good comes from coming." Motts paused, then briefly met Vina's eyes before they broke into giggles. "Go wake up the new lovebirds. The bacon's about done. And then I'll pop in the eggs to scramble them."

CHAPTER FIFTEEN

"Save me," Motts whispered to River, who sat on her left side. She knew ignoring the man on her right was rude but couldn't help herself. "I can't sit through dinner. I'll have a meltdown."

"Already finding a solution," her cousin murmured mysteriously. "Can you make it through appetisers?"

"Maybe."

Her auntie Lily was a lovely woman who enjoyed entertaining family and friends. She also had a nasty habit of trying to play matchmaker. Her efforts usually tended to be restricted to her son.

Unfortunately for Motts, her cousin River had begun dating Nish. Auntie Lily adored Nish, which was great. The downside, however, came in her love of matchmaking transferring to Motts.

Motts sunk deeper into her chair. She didn't know if dumplings, biangbiang noodles with garlic beef, and custard tart for dessert were worth the nightmare of making small talk with a stranger. *Make an effort. You can't sit here saying nothing.* "So, what do you do for a living, Edwin?"

"Dermot," her blind date corrected. "As I said earlier, I'm a journalist."

Bugger.

River, the traitorous berk, snickered under his breath. "Well done, Motts."

"I need air." Motts got to her feet and fled the room. She went out the back door to sit on the steps leading down to the garden. "Catastrophic colliding candid cabbages."

"Who's a cabbage?" Her uncle squeezed on the step next to her. He draped a jacket around her shoulders. "Your auntie wants you to be happy."

"I am," Motts grumbled. "Mostly. I'd be happier without someone chucking rocks through my window. And awkward and unexpected blind dates don't exactly fill me with joy either."

He wrapped an arm around her. "I did try to talk her out of the blind date."

"And?"

"Have you ever tried to convince Cactus not to roll around in catnip?"

"No." Motts peered up at him in confusion.

"Try it. And maybe you'll understand. Matchmaking is your auntie's catnip. She adores connecting couples." He squeezed her shoulders gently. "I'll talk to her. We want you to feel comfortable and welcome in our home. And you having to flee from the table during supper isn't alright."

"I'm sorry."

"No, love, we're sorry," her uncle argued immediately. "Want me to bring you dinner out here? It is delicious—I snuck a taste while we were making it together."

"Motts?"

She tilted her head around to see River standing in the doorway. "Yes?"

"You have a guest." He smiled mischievously at her. "Mum's adding a chair to the table. You *don't* want to miss this."

Her curiosity got the better of her. Motts followed her cousin and uncle into the house. She almost stumbled over her own feet when she spotted a familiar, intimidating figure seated next to Dermot with an empty spot on his other side.

Her aunt seemed incredibly happy. Dermot, on

the other hand, looked as if he'd rather be eating his dinner directly off a public restroom floor. And her cousin, of course, observed the chaos he'd created with a pleased grin.

Motts slid into her chair. *What is he even doing here?* "Detective Inspector. Do you often join random families for dinner? Or is this your first one?"

"Motts." Teo glanced down when she plucked a strand of knitting yarn off his jacket. "I was at my weekly knitting club meeting in Looe when someone texted about free dumplings. I never turn those down."

"Dumplings." Motts shook her head. "Wait. Why is your knitting club in Looe?"

"That's the part you find strange?" River grunted when she kicked his leg under the table. "Abuse."

Teo chose to ignore the bickering cousins and answer Motts's question. "My parents live here. The club was started by one of the nuns at their church. I take my mother every week."

Motts watched as her auntie practically melted. If she'd been one of the characters in a graphic novel, her eyes would've been literal hearts. "Not sure this was a good idea."

"I can leave." He leaned in to whisper to her.

"No." She kept her voice low. "Not sure Dermot agrees."

"Dermot is reassessing every life decision up until this point." Teo nodded.

The rest of the meal went smoothly, though a bit uncomfortably. Motts felt sorry for Dermot. She wondered what her auntie had told the poor man, who made his escape the second dessert had finished.

"I am sorry, darling." Auntie Lily looped her arm around Motts, leading her into the den. "The boys can clear the table off. We'll sit and chat about them."

"Motts has a date." River once again saved her from torture. He ushered her and Teo out the front door before his mum could argue. "Chat later. I'm sure the detective inspector can give you a ride home, since I picked you up."

"Your aunt is watching us from the front window." Teo followed her down the drive towards his vehicle. "Should I be concerned?"

Motts narrowed her eyes, trying to decide if he was joking or being serious. "I think you'll be safe. Don't give her your number. She has no idea how annoying group texts can be."

"Incredibly annoying."

Motts waited until they'd gotten on the road to Polperro to pose a question to Teo. "How exactly did my cousin get your number?"

. . .

"He was a witness to a crime."

"And you give all witnesses your personal number to text you invites to family dinners?" Motts didn't buy the excuse for a second. It made no sense. "Why do I have a feeling Nish and Vina have your number as well?"

"Witnesses to a crime."

"Did you give Doc your number? He witnessed my hit-and-run." Motts took his silence to mean he hadn't. "Precisely. So why my family?"

"I can't discuss police matters." Teo winked at her.

What does that mean?

The conversation moved to other topics. Motts thought she'd missed something. She had no idea what.

She wanted to ask Vina, who often played translator for her. Teo would probably wonder why she was texting. It could wait.

They sank into a comfortable quiet for the last few minutes of the drive. Motts found Teo was thankfully one of those people who didn't need to fill the silence. He dropped her off, waiting for her to close the door before driving off.

Motts leaned against the closed door and breathed in deeply. "What a strange evening. Cactus?"

Meow.

Her beloved cat prowled down the hall toward her.

He rubbed against her legs and followed her into the kitchen. She lifted him up into her arms.

"Would you like some tuna?" She opened the fridge to grab the package she'd picked up at the market. "There are a few bits left."

While Cactus finished his treat, Motts checked on Moss. Her turtle didn't seem overly excited to see her. She did move slowly to nosh on a raspberry.

How do you know if a turtle is excited?

Leaving philosophical questions for another day, Motts retreated to the guest room. She'd been slowly turning it into an office and workspace. All of her origami and quilling papers now lined the walls in baskets set on shelves.

A large desk sat in the middle of the room with a futon against the corner. Motts had gotten the pull-out sofa to replace the bed. She grabbed a stack of patterned papers and sat in the armchair she used instead of a proper office chair.

She had several orders for clients but also ones purely for the joy of creating. Her current quilling side project was a recreation of a red and gold sari. It had been Leena's wedding dress.

It was one of her most complicated and advanced quilling designs to date. Vina had gotten her photos of the original sari over a year ago. Motts intended to finish the project by December, if possible.

In an hour of working with quilling papers, she soothed away most of her tension. Her mind enjoyed the rhythm of placing the scrolls into the design. It was a grand, complicated game of art by number.

Meow.

Motts glanced down at Cactus, who circled around her legs, trying to get her attention. He knew not to jump onto her work table. "Okay, smart kitty. Is it past time for me to take a break?"

Meow.

"I'll take that as a yes." Motts carefully stored away her project and the quilling supplies. She never left anything out for curious kitties to peruse. "Why don't we watch the TRY channel? We can giggle together."

Cactus didn't laugh. He usually meowed and purred. Motts did like to think he enjoyed her company.

She grabbed a bar of Kernow's lemon meringue, craving sweets and white chocolate specifically. "Come on, Cactus. Let's get comfortable."

Grabbing a pair of cosy pyjamas, Motts changed quickly. Cactus had already curled up on his favourite pillow on her bed. She set up her laptop on the mattress and slipped under the covers.

Meow.

"I know. They're *hilarious*." Motts shifted around to stretch out on the bed on her side. She watched one video after the other until her eyes started to close. "Night, Cactus."

Meow.

"You're right. I should make sure all the doors are locked first."

CHAPTER SIXTEEN

"Did you hear the news?" Vina almost jumped across the counter at Motts when she walked into Griffin Brews. "Did you?"

"Have you overcaffeinated yourself again?" Motts blinked at her hyper ex-girlfriend. She knew Vina often taste-tested new coffee drinks before adding them to the menu. "Or tried too many sweet pastries?"

"I'm not sugared up."

"Okay." Motts didn't know if she agreed. "What news am I supposed to have heard?"

"Rose Walters was taken to the police station for questioning." Vina waved Motts closer, lowering her voice to avoid the customers seated at one of the round tables. "She was the hooded figure who tossed a rock through your window."

"Rose?"

"Rose."

"Rose Walters? The sweet lady who's married to the grumpiest man I've ever met?" Motts wondered how much caffeine Vina had ingested. "Are you sure?"

Rolling her eyes, Vina searched her pockets and pulled out her phone with a triumphant shout. She queued up a video she'd obviously taken. Motts watched as Inspector Ash and Constable Stone led Rose out of the Salty Seaman.

"I...." Motts trailed off, too stunned to complete her thought.

"Right? Hughie stopped by for a latte. He told me why they'd taken her in for questioning." Vina slipped her phone into her pocket. "Here. I'll make you a coffee."

"How is that going to help?"

"When doesn't coffee help?" Vina pointed out.

Taking a seat in the corner of the café, Motts fidgeted with her phone. She wondered how the police had identified Rose. Despite Vina's thoughts, she knew taking someone in for questioning wasn't the same as them actually being arrested.

Still, Motts couldn't help wondering why. What in the world would lead Rose to throw a stone through her cottage window? She'd welcomed Motts so kindly.

Was it all the questions about Rhona?

Vina brought over two mugs of coffee and a plate of breakfast pasties. She sat across from Motts. "Have you heard from Detective Inspector Tall, Dark, and Brooding?"

"We need an acronym for him." Motts picked at the flaky layers of the pasty. "He hasn't texted. I saw him yesterday."

"I heard all about it. River messaged Nish and me."

"Of course he did." She shook her head. "Marnie never mentioned the arrest when I dropped by to see her."

"Maybe she doesn't know." Vina shrugged.

"Possible." Motts dug into her pasty. She'd need the energy for her cycling adventure. "Can I fill my water bottle here? I'm cycling to Polruan. I'm going to make a circuit of it."

"Polruan? That's a good two hours or more of cycling, depending on how you go. Have you lost your mind?" Vina leaned forward to rest her palm against Motts's forehead. "You don't feel feverish."

"I'm fine. But I need to get going. I don't fancy cycling late in the afternoon. If I leave now, I'll have time to explore and get back to the cottage before it gets dark." Motts intended to go a little out of her way to Lantic Bay, or at least hike up to the top of the cliffs to enjoy the view. "Want to go?"

"Not even if we were still dating." She shook her head. "You're going to need snacks. Good snacks. Don't go anywhere."

"Vina," Motts groaned. Her ex-girlfriend had already disappeared, racing into the café's kitchen with Motts's water bottle in hand. "Brilliant."

Between Vina, Nish, and their parents, Motts wound up with overflowing saddlebags. She had the filled water bottle along with a range of travel-ready snacks. There was no way she could eat all the food they'd given to her.

Leena and Caden, in particular, had insisted on making sure her mobile phone had been charged. Caden turned very paternal. He gave her a local road map (in case her GPS stopped working), a tyre patch kit, and a fancy mini pump.

"I'm not cycling to the other side of the world." Motts waved off the Griffin parents' offer to pick her up in Polruan. "I'll be perfectly fine."

"Don't hesitate to give us a ring if you change your mind." Leena hugged her tightly.

I'm not leaving forever.

Motts had learned over the years from painfully

embarrassing moments not to blurt out all of her thoughts. "Thanks."

When in doubt, a one-word response tended to keep her safe from making a mistake. Motts endured the well-meaning advice and hugs. She cycled out of sight as soon as possible.

Heading west out of the village, she took mostly smaller roads, going left by a farm and stopping for a flock of sheep. The wee lambs made her smile.

About three-quarters of the way to Polruan, Motts eased off the road onto a dirt path. She made her way on foot, pushing her bike up the hill. The view at the top of the cliff had definitely been worth the effort.

Dodging one of the cows munching on the grass, Motts wandered over to one of the trees along the clifftop. She rested her bike against the trunk, grabbed her bottle of water, and sat on the grass to stare out across the bay and sea. The wind whipped her hair around her face and cooled her off.

I needed this.

A peaceful calm settled over Motts. She didn't always enjoy being out in nature with her allergies. But every so often, cycling less crowded routes offered a rare opportunity to relax without having to engage in conversation.

Nothing stressed Motts as much as small talk.

The dinner at her auntie and uncle's had been a total nightmare even with Teo coming to the rescue. People always expected a conversation to flow smoothly.

And she frequently wanted to not have to talk.

At all.

Cows definitely didn't require a chat. Motts sat for almost an hour up on the hill. She'd set a timer for herself to keep from staying too long.

Snacks.

I have snacks.

Motts dug into her saddlebag and grabbed half a sandwich. She peeled apart the bread, eating the cheddar and thinly sliced beef separately. "The bicycle isn't going to take itself home."

Walking back down the path to the road, Motts had time to let her snack settle before climbing onto the bike. She'd spent a little longer than intended by the sea but not by much. There was plenty of time to explore Polruan before heading home.

After a warm mug of tea at Crumpets, Motts meandered around the village for an hour. She'd planned to start the journey home no later than two in the afternoon. The grey clouds beginning to fill the sky changed her mind.

I can't believe I forget to check the weather. What a

silly mistake to make. I'm going to get soaked through to the bone.

Pulling out her phone, Motts entered her cottage into the map and picked the most direct route home. She had a feeling the rain would arrive before she got there. Her legs weren't prepared for a full-on sprint for an hour.

Halfway down the road to Polperro, the skies opened above her. Motts wound up drenched within ten minutes. She cursed herself for not checking the weather more closely in the morning.

Several cars beeped when they passed her on the road. Motts didn't understand the point. She was fully aware her life decisions had let her down.

She hadn't missed the fact it was raining. It streaked down her face and made keeping her cycling straight more complicated. She briefly considered making a rude gesture at the next driver who thought it was funny to drive through a puddle next to her.

Why are people such jerks?

A vehicle pulled up beside her about twenty minutes from home. Nish hopped out and helped her get her bicycle into the back of the delivery van. She climbed into the front, shivering in her damp clothes.

Nish slipped into the driver seat. He reached over

to turn up the heat. "Let's get you home so you can get into dry clothes."

"Thanks, Nish." Motts took the towel he tossed to her and dried her face. She'd been looking forward to cycling along the coast. "It didn't seem stormy earlier in the day."

"Did you enjoy your day, aside from the sudden onslaught of rain?" Nish pointed to a thermos on the console between them. "Amma sent some tea. She thought you might appreciate the warmth."

Motts poured herself a cup, managing to keep from spilling it when Nish went over a bump in the road. "I spent some time on the cliffs about Lantic Bay. It was lovely. The rain, not so much."

Sipping the tea, Motts tried not to shatter her teeth shivering. The cold had definitely begun to sink into her bones. She'd be heading straight for a hot bath the minute she got home.

Nish guided the van up the road to park outside her cottage. He took the finished thermos cup from her. "Here. I'll get your bike secured. You get inside and warm yourself. I'm sure one of us will check in on you later. Maybe bring up some stew or soup for supper."

Cactus was sitting by the front door when Motts finally got her fingers to work enough to turn the key in the lock. She waved at Nish before shutting the door. Her clothes dripped a trail of water down the hall into the bathroom.

Meow.

"Yes, I'm aware I've left a mess in my wake." Motts got the water in the tub going. She stripped out of her wet clothes, tossing them into the laundry basket in the corner. They could wait until later. "Just one of my many mistakes today."

Grabbing a spare towel, Motts dropped it and shuffled around on her feet to dry the floor. Cactus didn't need to catch a cold as well. She finished up just as the bath had filled.

Motts climbed into the tub and sank into the blissfully hot water. She rested her head against the edge. The warmth felt like the best hug in the world.

Meow.

"I'll feed you as soon as I stop shivering like it's forty below outside." Motts reached out to rub Cactus on the head. He leapt up to sit on the shelf at the foot of the tub to watch her. "Do not jump into the water."

Cactus had made the mistake more than once. He wanted to join her and always managed to look as if she'd betrayed him when his little paws hit the water. Motts sat forward to dislodge him to a safer spot.

Turning his tail up, Cactus strolled out of the bathroom. She had a feeling she'd need a few extra treats to get on his good side again. That was a problem for later, when her body had stopped acting like she'd gone for a dive in the sea on a winter morning.

She reclined back in the tub and let out a heavy sigh. "Well, who says going outdoors is good for you?"

CHAPTER SEVENTEEN

The following morning, Motts struggled to get out of bed. She curled under the covers to keep warm until her stomach and Cactus protested too loudly to ignore. *Brunch it is.*

She'd barely sat down with her usual toast with lemon curd and a large mug of coffee when the doorbell rang. She grumbled all the way to the door, lifting Cactus up to keep him from running outside. "Inspector Ash. Up early."

He glanced down at his watch. "It's near eleven."

"You're up *here* at my cottage early." Motts hadn't even changed out of her pyjamas. She coughed against Cactus to keep from doing it in the inspector's face. "Something wrong?"

"Can I come in?"

No?

I'm in my pyjamas. My toast is getting weirdly soft. My coffee is definitely cooling off. And Cactus might claw my face off for coughing against his skin.

No.

No?

Can I tell a police inspector to go away? Close the door?

Oh my god, say something before he thinks you need your brain rebooted.

"Okay." Motts twisted around, not bothering to invite him inside. She set Cactus on the couch and returned to the table to finish her toast. "Is this about Rose?"

Inspector Ash nodded. "She's admitted to lobbing the stone through the window."

"I don't understand why." Motts picked at the crust on her toast. "She treated me so kindly the few times I met her."

"She refuses to answer our questions outside of admitting to having committed the vandalism. She'll likely be fined and told to pay the damages. It's her first offence. I doubt she's going to see any further punishment." He stood uncomfortably for a minute, then finally sat down when Motts continued to casually eat her toast. "I didn't want you to wonder if you saw her in the village."

"Was she trying to deter me from asking questions about Rhona's disappearance?"

"Let us handle the investigation."

Motts squished a piece of crust between her fingers. "Was she protecting herself or Innis?"

"Ms Mottley." Inspector Ash bent forward with his elbows on the table. "We are competent detectives. We won't rest until we have answers. Please don't insert yourself any further into the investigation."

"Of course. Can I see you out?" Motts liked Marnie; she thought the bridal shop owner's husband needed a lot of work. "It's lovely to see you."

It's not.

Please, please go away so I can finish my toast.

The inspector left. He seemed bemused by her rushing him out the door. Motts tried to settle in to finally finish her brunch.

Shoving her plate away, she gave up on the toast. She hated when it got too soft from the lemon curd. Her mind kept turning to the mystery of Rose and the stone.

Why?

Why would she lob a stone through Motts's window? Had it been in defence of Innis? Was she trying to scare Motts away from asking any more questions?

Trying to stop her from probing too deeply into their family's history? Or was she trying to protect herself? If that was the case, what motive had Rose had to hurt Rhona?

In the end, Motts supposed both Rose and Innis had the same motive. They'd suffer equally if the Salty Seaman had been sold out from under them. Money tempted even the saintliest of people to commit terrible crimes.

"Want to go visit Auntie Vina and Uncle Nish?" Motts decided a special mug of tea from Griffin Brews was in order. It usually made her feel loads better. The weather was still cool enough for Cactus to be able to venture out with her. "Let's get your little T-shirt on."

Before taking Cactus outside, Motts checked on her bicycle. It had dried off after the rain the previous day. She set up a cushion in the basket on the front for her beloved cat.

"Ready to be spoiled?" Motts secured him into the basket. She'd fashioned a seat belt, of sorts, for him. "I'm sure Granny Leena will be thrilled to be graced with your presence."

Cycling down the hill, Motts rode more carefully with her precious cargo. She parked outside Griffin

Brews and lifted Cactus up to wave at Nish through the glass. He rushed out to snatch Cactus from her arms.

"We'll be in the office." Nish dashed through the café, much to her amusement.

"What did you do to my brother?" Vina greeted her when she stepped up to the counter.

"He had Cactus," Motts explained. She glanced at the board for new options. "Do you have your masala chai blend? My throat is sore."

"I've got one with extra ginger. We'll add a dash of honey to help." Vina reached for the special mug they kept just for Motts. "Why don't I get you one of Amma's pumpkin and saffron sugar spiced pasties?"

"Will it help my throat?"

"Sure." Vina grinned. "Marnie popped by earlier. She said Rose would be home by the end of the day. She sent Perry to warn you."

"Inspector Ash stopped by already." Motts wondered if Marnie had meant the warning to be different than the one she received. "Don't think he approves of me."

"Who wouldn't approve of you? You're brilliant." Vina busied herself making the tea. She spooned in a decent amount of honey. She stirred vigorously, then slid the mug across the counter. "I'll get you the pastry.

Why don't you head into the office? Cactus won't want to be without you for long."

"If he's seen your mum, he won't even notice me." Motts grabbed the mug and followed Vina through the swinging doors. She waved at Caden, who was elbows deep into whipping up some sort of dough. "Hello."

"Did she get you sorted with breakfast?"

"I wouldn't let our Motts starve, Dad." Vina protested. "Honestly. I'm offended you think I'd ignore her needs."

"I'm ignoring you both." Motts left the father and daughter duo to pretend to argue with each other. She knew from experience they could be a while. Nish and his mum were fawning over Cactus in the small café office. "Are you spoiling him?"

"Amma's idea." Nish pointed to his mum, who was feeding Cactus by hand. "She made treats especially for him. It's all cat safe. Promise."

"As though I would *ever* even dream of feeding this little angel anything that might hurt him." She kissed Cactus on the head, murmuring to him in Punjabi. Her attention returned to Motts. "Are you well? Chai with honey? Are you sick? I'll make my chicken soup for you to take home."

Motts blinked as Leena disappeared in a swirl of her sari, a deep purple silk with gold embroidery. She wore them often; usually, according to her, on days when she wanted to feel extra beautiful. Nish snickered at Motts's dumbfounded expression. "Quit laughing at me."

"One of these days you'll believe my parents think you're their third child. And their favourite," he teased. "Guess who has another date with your cousin?"

"No idea." Motts sipped her tea, allowing the warmth to coat and soothe her throat. She felt almost an immediate relief. "Brilliant. So, who's River going on a date with?"

"Me." Nish shook his head. "You're hopeless."

"No, I'm autistic, and sometimes I think you're joking when you're being serious." Motts shrugged. She dipped her pastry into the tea and took a quick bite. "I have a question."

"Yes, they're practising safe sex." Vina squeezed into the office and chuckled when Motts wrinkled her nose. "We don't all find it repulsive."

"I'm uninterested. Not repulsed," Motts corrected. She believed people shouldn't play around with words and labels that meant something. "I'm serious. I have a question."

"We're all ears." Vina sat on the edge of the desk and stole Cactus from her brother. "Not literally, figuratively, if you were wondering."

Motts ignored the teasing. "Do we think Rose is capable of murder? Or is she protecting Innis, who definitely seems like the type?"

"Agree completely with your assessment of Innis." Vina stroked Cactus's head like a supervillain from a movie. "Rose might be capable. She certainly killed your window."

"Hilarious." Nish retrieved Cactus and stepped over to the other side of the office. He stared out the window. "Maybe she *thinks* Innis did something?"

"Or maybe they were both involved?" Vina joined her brother by the window. "I'd say Rose was released by the police. She's rushing down the street now as if she's being chased by the detective."

Stepping up between the twins, Motts watched the drama unfolding down the street. Rose and Innis were definitely having an argument in full view of anyone who could see through the windows of their fish and chip shop. She'd love to be a fly on the wall.

Nish reached out to crack the office window. "I can't hear what they're saying."

They all went quiet when Rose stormed out of the Salty Seaman. Innis locked the door behind her. They stood on either side, continuing to yell at each other.

Motts leaned forward to try to hear what the

couple were shouting. "Would it be too obvious if we went outside and checked on my bike?"

"Definitely." Vina nodded.

The three exchanged glances before rushing out of the office. They dashed through the kitchen, ignoring Caden's complaints. The trio slowed down to a walk when they made it to the front of the café.

Motts made a show of checking her tyres while Vina and Nish placed Cactus in his basket. "Bugger. They've noticed us."

And they had. The sound of footsteps made Motts stand up straight. She shook her head when the twins moved to block her from view.

"She's not going to stone me in the middle of Polperro," Motts muttered. "I hope. I'm certain the police would frown on it. Isn't stoning against the law?"

"That's what you're worried about?" Nish twisted around to whisper at her.

"What? I'm curious."

"Your mind is such an interesting place." Nish shook his head. Motts moved up beside him, and he wrapped his arm around her shoulders. They made a combined front when Rose finally reached them. "Rose."

"I'm sorry for breaking your window." Rose didn't

seem especially sorry. She appeared quite angry to Motts. "We'll pay for the damage."

"Why'd you do it?" Vina asked the question Motts had been attempting to form.

"I've apologised. I'm paying to fix the window." Rose drew herself up, shoving her hands into the pockets of her cardigan. "Why is irrelevant."

"It's not, actually," Vina disagreed.

Motts placed a hand on Vina's arm. She could tell her ex-girlfriend was starting to get a little heated over the obviously unapologetic apology. "I'd like to understand what drove you to vandalise my home."

"Maybe if you'd learn to mind your own business, things like that wouldn't happen." Rose stormed away from them, returning to bang on the door until Innis let her inside.

Motts glanced between her two friends and back over to the Salty Seaman. She could see Innis and Rose were still arguing through the window. "I don't think Innis knew about her throwing stones."

"Why do I get the feeling their day is about to get worse?" Nish drew their attention to the police vehicle pulling up to the fish and chip shop. Constable Stone and Inspector Ash climbed out, heading over to the door. "Wait. Why are they grabbing Innis?"

"The plot has thickened." Vina spoke the words

Motts had been thinking. "Maybe you were right about Rose trying to draw attention away from her husband?"

"Maybe."

Gossip in a small village worked faster than bees pollinating a garden. Nish popped by later in the evening with leftover stew from his mum. He also came bearing news about Innis.

The fish and chip shop owner had been taken in for questioning in regards to the disappearance of his sister. One of their guesses about Rose's motivation had been correct. She'd wanted to draw attention away from her husband.

She obviously believed he'd been involved in Rhona's death. It didn't surprise her that the police had wanted to ask Innis a few questions. Nish didn't know if they'd be able to hold him beyond twenty-four hours.

"They won't." Motts put half of the stew into a bowl and set the rest aside. She'd save it for leftovers. "Want some?"

"Think positively, Motts. Innis might confess. Or take a swing at Perry and get himself locked up for a little longer." Nish waved off her offer of food. "Want me to make tea?"

"Sure." She stirred her food around absently,

trying to draw courage to tell him a secret. "I have a date."

"An actual date?"

"Yes." Motts stared down at her stew. "Maybe? I was invited to go to the Kernow chocolate factory."

"By a man? Woman? Easter bunny?"

"Easter bunny?" She carried her bowl into the living room to sit on the couch. Nish followed, flopping down beside her. "A man."

"A man I know?"

"Yes."

"Do we have to play twenty questions?" Nish stole a chunk of meat from her bowl. "Wait. Is it the detective from Plymouth? Please say it's him. He's a dish and a half. River told me about his coming to the rescue after the disaster of a blind date."

Motts nodded. "He sent me an email inviting me to the factory."

"An email?"

"An email." Motts didn't know if email invitations counted as dates. They didn't know each other incredibly well yet. "Maybe it's a platonic sort of thing?"

"Show me the message." Nish took her phone when she handed it over to read the email. "We're going to need reinforcements. I have no idea."

Reinforcements meant talking River and Vina into

coming over. Motts sat on the couch, eating stew and observing the trio. They read the email from Teo over and over to debate the nuances of his wording.

When their debate got a little too excited, Motts decided it was time to have her cottage to herself. Nish corralled the other two out the door with him. He waved at her before closing the door behind them.

Right.

I have the entire night to stress about whether or not Teo meant it.

Motts took consolation from the fact her non-autistic friends were just as confused. "What do you think, Cactus?"

Meow.

"You're right. I might as well ask him." Motts didn't see much point in dancing around issues. She wanted to understand, and no one else seemed to have answers. "Straight from the horse's mouth. What does it even mean? Straight from the horse's mouth. Horses can't talk."

CHAPTER EIGHTEEN

"I feel like I'm sitting outside of the headmistress's office, waiting to be told off for something I didn't do." Motts had eaten toast, drunk far too much coffee, fed her animals, and now waited on the sofa for Teo to arrive. "What do I do, Cactus? I can't practice every possible conversation we might have."

He ignored her. Vina had brought a catnip-filled toy for him earlier when she'd come to give Motts a pep talk. He'd been playing with it ever since.

Despite having spent three hours stressing over being ready on time, Teo arrived, and Motts immediately spilt tea all over her jumper. She let him inside, then ran down the hall into her bedroom to change. Cactus could entertain the detective.

"Are you communing with my cat?" Motts stared

at Teo, who had Cactus gently held in both hands. The two were staring each other down face-to-face. "I'm ready to go. Or do you need to play 'don't blink' with my cat for a little longer?"

"He started it." Teo continued to hold Cactus up so their noses were almost touching. "He was sitting next to your turtle's home, meowing."

"They're friends. They gossip."

Teo tilted his head, and his gaze shifted from Cactus to her. "They gossip?"

"Yes." Motts nodded. She tugged at her jumper slightly; making sure it covered her T-shirt underneath. "Are we going?"

Teo set Cactus down on the cushion next to Moss's terrarium. "Do they gossip often?"

"Define often."

Teo's lips twitched, but he didn't smile. "Let's get going. I spoke to the tour coordinator at Kernow. They don't have anyone scheduled for an early morning tour. I figured you'd rather not be shoved into a massive group of strangers."

He wasn't wrong. Motts appreciated his kind gesture. She double-checked the locks, security system, and her pets before following him out of the cottage.

"They'll be fine," Teo promised when Motts locked her front door for the fourth time. "You've got the app on your phone. You can check on the cottage anytime you like."

"I'm being silly." She shoved her keys into her pocket, wincing when one of them dug into her side. "Silly sad salty sandwich."

"You're not being silly." Teo opened the passenger door for her. He winked when she frowned at him. "You have every reason to be concerned, given how your first weeks in Cornwall went."

The tour of the chocolate factory went by quickly. Teo seemed bemused by how fast Motts observed and moved forward. She didn't see a point in taking forever.

Her mum had stopped going to museums with her because of how swiftly Motts moved through the exhibits. Once she'd seen something, she didn't get any further enjoyment by standing and staring for minutes on end. What did it matter, as long as she had fun?

Fun wasn't measured with a specific timeframe, was it?

They spent most of their time by the taste-test table. Motts had a feeling their tour guide hadn't expected them to eat their way through everything offered. They didn't want the chocolate to go to waste.

By the time they left, Motts had bought more

chocolate than was probably wise. Teo couldn't comment. He'd gotten more than she had.

"Is there a chocolates anonymous? I'm thinking we might be addicts." Motts held up her bag. "I could concuss someone with this."

"We've got an hour before lunch. Why don't we check out the bookshop?" Teo stored their bags in the boot of his vehicle. "It's not too far."

They drove further into Wadebridge, parked, and walked the rest of the way. Motts wasn't wound up in book shops unless they had a decent graphic novel section. She didn't mind checking out a new one, though.

To her surprise, Motts managed to find a handful of graphic novels she didn't have. *The Inflatable Woman* by Rachel Ball had been on her to-be-read list for a while. She left the shop with more books than Teo, much to his amusement.

Grabbing a coffee on the way, they walked through the village to Le Snack, a takeaway sandwich place. Teo had apparently determined it would be a safe choice for lunch. She got chicken breast with pesto on a baguette along with chips.

There were more people out and about. Motts's nerves were starting to feel a little frayed around the edges. Teo suggested they make the walk back to his vehicle.

Once there, Teo drove outside of the city to a parking area along the River Camel. They had a brilliant view while chowing down on their lunch. Motts appreciated the quiet, confined space without being inundated by the constant noise of other people.

"Do you think Innis killed his sister?" Motts picked a slice of tomato from her sandwich. She munched on it, watching Teo out of the corner of her eye. "People will do strange things when money is involved. They tend to lose all sense of reality."

Teo finished chewing his bite of jacket potato. He sipped some of his water. "I can't answer."

"I don't want a copy of your case file or a debrief on the interrogation." She went for a slice of cucumber next, crunching her way through it. "What do your trained instincts say?"

"Aside from needing you to stop watching crime shows on the telly?" He frowned at her thoughtfully. "I'm waiting to see if the evidence convinces me."

"I don't watch the telly," Motts insisted. She went back to eating her sandwich in separate pieces. "I like true crime podcasts."

"Podcasts?"

"I can listen to them while I'm working. And I can rewind them when I don't hear things right." Motts hated her occasional inability to process sound. She often had to restart her podcasts several times or pause them until her brain had caught up. "If you're waiting to be convinced by the evidence, his interrogation either didn't go well or made you think he might be innocent."

Teo tossed a handful of chips into his mouth. He chewed slowly, probably to give himself time to think of an answer. "You don't have much of a poker face, but you're damned perceptive. Ask me in a few days, and I'll be able to give you an answer."

"Alright." Motts shrugged. She didn't see a reason to push the detective inspector for an answer. It would only ruin what had been a lovely day. "I enjoyed our friendly outing."

"But you've run out of energy for outside stimulation?"

"What?"

"Something that my cousin says when she's reached her limit of being around people." Teo took the last bite of his sandwich. He wiped his hands clean and gathered all the trash into the paper packet the food had come in. "We can head back now if you like."

Reaching over to turn on the radio, Teo found a classical music station. They drove the fifty minutes to her cottage mostly in pleasant silence. She wanted to thank him for a brilliant day, but her nerves had picked up again the closer to home they got.

"Was this a date or a friend thing?" Motts asked the question she'd been practising in her head since yesterday.

"It's whatever you feel comfortable with it being." Teo pulled up in front of her cottage. He shut the engine off, then twisted slightly towards her. "I'll leave the decision up to you. I should tell you something first, though."

"You're a vampire?"

"What?" he asked, sounding wholly bewildered.

"Just wondering." She grinned.

"No, I find having this conversation to be uncomfortable but necessary before entering even a casual relationship." He tapped his finger against the steering wheel with an uncharacteristic show of nervousness. "I'm not trying to make you uneasy."

She simply nodded in response.

"I'm asexual."

Motts stared. And stared. She snorted, then giggled, much to her embarrassment. "Is that all?"

"Tends to be a deal breaker." He sounded as though he spoke from a lot of painful experience.

"I suppose now is the time I play my own ace card."

"What?"

Motts stretched the sleeves of her jumper, covering her hands. "We have something in common beyond our love of chocolate."

"Oh. *Oh.*" His lips quirked up into a smile. "That makes this is far less awkward than usual."

Neither of them seemed to know where to go with the conversation. Motts hopped out, grabbed her items from the boot, muttered a thanks, and raced into her cottage. She sank down to the floor by the front door after closing it.

"Oh, boy," she groaned. Cactus made his way over to her, butting his head against her leg. "Hello, sweetheart, did you have a good day? I brought you some of my chicken sandwich."

Meow.

"I did have a good day."

After spending an evening recovering from her date, Motts woke the next morning to insistent knocking on her door. She grabbed her phone and found several missed calls. Cactus followed her through the cottage to the front door, where she found Nish, River, and Vina waiting impatiently.

"We brought coffee. The good kind. And we've got

full English breakfast pasties." River pushed into the cottage past her. Vina and Nish wrapped their arms around Motts to guide her after him. "Now, sing for your supper."

"He's had a few coffees already," Nish whispered.

They gathered around her kitchen table. Motts picked apart her pasty. Cactus ran off with a large chunk of bacon from the filling.

"Cheeky bugger."

"Is he cheeky when you literally handed the bacon to him?" Vina asked around a mouthful of pasty. She grabbed one of the coffees in the centre of the table. "Cactus is not the bloke we want to talk about."

Meow.

"You've offended him." Motts watched Cactus leap up onto the windowsill to stare out into the garden. "He'll be insufferable later."

"*Mottsy.*" Vina had never been a patient person. "Tell us about your date."

"Pravina." Nish kicked his sister's chair. "We have talked about demanding things from people."

"Spoilsport," Vina muttered. "Sorry, Mottsy."

She chuckled at the siblings, exchanging a grin with her cousin. "I brought you all chocolate from Kernow."

"Sod the chocolate. What about the man?" Vina

leaned forward with her elbows on the table. "Do we need to hunt him down and dump him in a river?"

"He was brilliant." Motts hid her smile behind her cup of coffee. She held it tightly, enjoying the warmth. "We got chocolate, went to a bookshop, and had sandwiches."

"And?" River prompted.

And?

She didn't really know what they wanted to hear. They'd gotten a play-by-play of her day out with the detective inspector. At most, it had been a friendly sort of first date; they'd agreed not to put any pressure on themselves.

"Motts?"

She gave a confused shrugged. "I had a nice time."

"We're glad." Nish interrupted both Vina and River, who'd started to ask questions. "Aren't we?"

"He's like me." Motts finally offered a little more information for the infuriatingly curious trio.

"Like...." Vina's eyebrows went up in surprise. "Is he now? Well, how nice."

Motts turned towards her ex-girlfriend in surprise. "You sound strange."

"She's fine." Nish once again nudged his sister, who nodded rapidly. "See?"

"Not really." Motts felt increasingly uneasy. She

pushed her plate away and clung to her cup of coffee. "Do you not like him?"

"She—"

"Nish," Vina snapped at her brother. She reached out to take Motts's hand and hold it gently. "I think Detective Inspector Broody will be perfect for you. I'm jealous he's better for you than I was."

"You've got a girlfriend. And we haven't been together for ages." Motts didn't understand jealousy in general, but this definitely confused her. "I don't get why you'd be upset."

"I'm not. I am genuinely happy for you, even if he turns out to be just a friend. Whatever happens." Vina squeezed her hand, then leaned back into her chair. "Ignore my momentary blip."

"Okay," Motts said uncertainly.

After breakfast, her friends headed off to work, leaving her alone in the cottage. Vina had hung back to ensure Motts knew she was genuinely delighted. The weird little blip of conversation still confused Motts, but she decided not to stress over it.

Setting a timer for herself, Motts rushed around the cottage cleaning up. She often struggled to force herself to keep up with housework. Twenty-minute increments helped to keep her on task.

With her cleaning done for the day, Motts moved

on to things she enjoyed doing. An order had come in from Etsy for a unique quilling project. She'd promised to make a miniature test to see if the idea was solid.

Three hours later, a meowing Cactus drew her attention away from concept design of an old ship being taken over by a Kraken. Motts stretched her arms out and unfolded her legs. She'd gotten too wrapped up in her excitement over the project and forgotten to have a tea break.

Cactus was usually great at reminding her to get up and move around. They shared a biscuit and tea. Motts rewarded him with a walk in the garden, checking on her plot of herbs and refilling the bird feeder.

Meow.

"Yes, they are hungry little feathery buggers, aren't they?" Motts yanked him into her arms when she heard footsteps on the trail leading by her garden down to the coastal walking path. *Meow.* "Sorry."

A few seconds later, Noel Watson strode down the trail. He froze when he spotted her by the bird feeder. Motts didn't say anything, just watched him pick up the pace and continue on out of view.

Odd.

Why had Noel been so shocked to see her standing

in her own garden? Made no sense. She couldn't recall seeing him on the coastal path in the month or so she'd been living in the cottage.

I'm getting way too suspicious. Not everyone is planning something nefarious. Nefarious. Nefariously nauseating numpties never nag.

Meow.

"Yes, let's go inside." Motts carried Cactus into the cottage. She locked the door, checking the bolt twice. "I'm perfectly safe. Noel's been a little standoffish, but I can be as well."

Setting Cactus down, Motts grabbed her mobile and went through the screens on the security app. No one. *I'm being daft. Stop it. You'll drive yourself to distraction if you keep on like this. You're perfectly safe in the cottage.*

She shook off her nerves and decided to make another cup of tea. One led to a second. She began to feel better after warming up.

Meow.

"I am being silly, sorry, sweetheart." Motts grabbed a treat and offered it to Cactus, who immediately pounced. She took a chunk of fruit over for Moss. "Hello, lovely, what's new in your world?"

Nothing, apparently.

She tried to get back to playing with her scrolled

paper. Nothing worked. Her mind kept straying to the look Noel had sent her way.

Motts didn't want to go out. She also didn't want to stay inside the cottage. Being alone had come with unexpected side effects, like jumping at every shadow.

CHAPTER NINETEEN

After a night of uneasy sleep, Motts woke to a welcome visitor with unwelcome news. Vina had stopped by with her favourite tea, scones, and a new jar of lemon curd. She'd also brought news from River, who'd overheard his dad and Motts's talking about her parents planning another trip out to Cornwall.

Because what Motts really needed was another round of parental intrusion. *I love Mum and Dad. It's all going to be okay. Take a few deep breaths. They won't stay for long. You'll have your space to yourself again.*

They got comfortable in the living room. Motts had two scones completely drowning in lemon curd. She sipped tea happily and smiled at Cactus, who was pestering Vina for a bite of her bacon sandwich.

"Mottsy."

"What?" Motts covered her mouth to keep scone crumbs from flying out. "Sorry."

Vina offered Cactus a tiny chunk of bacon. "Listen, yesterday, I don't know why I had a sudden burst of jealousy. When we broke up, I worried about you so much. And, I think, I thought I could somehow make up for abandoning you. For wanting more."

"We broke up because we both deserved to be happy in a romantic relationship. It was mutual. I love you. You're one of my best friends." Motts hadn't known Vina had held on to any guilt. "I'm not sad about breaking up."

Vina shook her head slowly and broke into loud laughter. "Your blunt honesty is both refreshing and surprising."

"So, we're okay, right?"

"Yep. Still best friends. I'm happy we've both found someone who might be perfect for us." Vina pushed Cactus back when he tried to steal more of her sandwich. "We *both* deserve to be happy."

"And you're done being weird?"

"Probably not." Vina smiled at her. "I am done being weird about you and Detective Inspector Broody."

"He's not broody. He smiles. I saw him," Motts insisted.

"What are you going to do about your parents?" Vina changed the subject and deftly deflected Cactus's reaching paw.

"Not open the door?"

"Motts."

"It might work." Motts crumbled up the last of her scone with an irritated huff. "I love Mum and Dad. Why can't they allow me to settle into my cottage? They've already been to see me. We talk and email."

"Maybe they want a vacation?"

She stared towards Vina. "A vacation? To Cornwall? Twice in a month?" Shaking off her annoyance, Motts decided not to dwell on the issue. She couldn't stop her parents from showing up. They'd likely already left London; she was going to have a long chat with them about surprise visits.

They knew she hated surprises. They claimed to understand how much changes in her routine disrupted her life. It caused her stress levels and blood pressure to rise to dangerously high levels.

Finishing up their breakfast, Vina headed off to the café to start work. Motts sat down to make a list. When her mind wanted to spiral into a panic, she found jotting down her thoughts on paper helped massively.

Most days.

Today was not a good day. Motts finished her list. She stared at it while staying curled up on the couch with Cactus watching her anxiously.

She forgot to have lunch. And shower. She didn't accomplish anything on her to-do list.

The day went by in a blur of staring out the window at the wind blowing through her garden. Cactus stayed by her side, ever her faithful shadow and protector. He only left to eat some of the food she'd left in his dish.

Some days, Motts truly hated the way her mind reacted to a sudden change, or even just the idea of it. She didn't move when someone knocked on her door. The banging became incessant, and her phone began to ring as well.

"Motts? I'm coming in. Using the key you gave me. Please don't be dead. Or dead and naked. Or just naked," River yelled through the door. She heard him putting the key in and opening the door. "Wherefore art thou, cousin of mine?"

Meow.

"Hello, naked kitten. Where's your mum?" River greeted Cactus. He carried him into the living room. "Oh good, you're not dead or naked."

Motts shrugged.

"Right." River placed Cactus gently into her lap. He sat on the coffee table in front of her, reaching over to pick up her notepad with the to-do list. "Ah. Did executive dysfunction shoot you with a freeze ray again?"

"A little."

River glanced down at her list that included a few things she wanted from the shops. "How about I help you knock a few of these out? If nothing else, you'll have less to stress over." Her cousin didn't wait for a response. He pulled out his mobile phone and texted the grocery items to Nish. And then he moved into the kitchen to start on the dishes.

An hour later, Nish showed up with milk, some veg and fruit, and other necessities. He and River busied themselves getting the kitchen clean. Nish had also brought a tea cake for her to serve to her parents.

Motts managed to pull herself out of her funk eventually. She was so grateful to her cousin and Nish for their help. They'd cleaned the kitchen, gotten her laundry out of the washer and out to dry in the sunshine. River had also gotten the futon set up with sheets and a blanket. "Thank you both so much."

River sat on the couch beside her. He wrapped an arm around her shoulders. "We love you. My dad said he'd chat with yours about this unexpected visiting business. They know better. Now, we've got a hot date. So, you relax and enjoy not having a long to-do list hanging over you like storm clouds."

Kissing her on the top of the head, River left with Nish following. They'd managed to knock most of the cleaning chores off her list, including taking out the rubbish. She only had to shower and take care of Moss and Cactus.

All I have to do is turn on the water. The warmth will feel lovely. The soap smells brilliant.

I can do this.

If I shower, I can enjoy the evening before they get here.

Just turn the water on.

It took a little convincing. Motts talked herself into getting up. She made herself walk down the hall to the bathroom and twist the handles to get the water to the perfect temperature.

With the water running, Motts had to shower. She didn't want to waste it. Cactus sat on the laundry basket in the corner and observed her.

Her quick shower helped to shake off the funk she'd sunken into. It always amazed her how much standing under warm water could help clear her mind. Did it work every time? No, but she'd take what she could get.

Motts dried off, then raided her wardrobe for her most comfortable clothing. She settled better in her warm penguin pyjama bottoms and an oversized graphic T-shirt. Vina had bought both for her a few years ago for her birthday.

The T-shirt had a large origami flower on the front. Motts wandered back to the kitchen with Cactus following. She fixed a fresh bowl for Cactus and diced up an array of fruit and veggies for Moss.

Her cousin, bless him, had done a fantastic job in her kitchen. Motts made a mental note to find a way to repay the two of them. Her mother would definitely have noticed all of the dirty dishes in the sink.

Inspecting all the items Nish had brought with him, Motts found a covered dish with some sort of curry. He'd also gotten her some fresh rolls. There was enough for her parents if they arrived in time for supper.

Her parents didn't call once, not shocking given they'd intended the trip to be a surprise. Motts could've phoned them to see where they were, but she didn't want to clue them into River's brilliant eavesdropping skills.

They arrived late in the evening. Motts had nibbled her way through two rolls and a portion of the curry. Her nerves had manifested into a desire to eat everything in the fridge.

It was almost eleven when her parents drove up to her cottage. Motts tried to summon a smile for them. Her dad's chuckle told her that she probably hadn't been completely successful.

"Hello, poppet." Her dad dragged her into a hug, bending down to rest his chin on top of her hand. "I tried talking her out of the trip. She threatened to come by herself."

Motts tried not to get annoyed. Her mum had always supported her through all of the ups and downs of school and afterwards starting her origami business. She'd just hoped for a little space to settle. "Are you staying long?"

"Only a few days." He laughed again at her relieved sigh. "No need to panic. We're not going to force our presence on you for weeks on end."

"Dad."

"Despite appearances, we are proud of you for going off on your own." He stepped away to allow her mum to embrace her tightly. "We heard you had a date."

I take back all the kind things I said about River.

"I had to hear about you and the detective

inspector from your auntie Lily. She gloated," her mum complained.

I doubt it.

Motts held her tongue and led her parents into the house. "Are you hungry? Nish brought over a curry earlier. There's plenty left for you both. It's not too spicy either."

"We're not fussy, darling." Her mum wandered into the kitchen.

Motts rolled her eyes as her mum inspected everything carefully. She forgave River for spilling the details of her date to Auntie Lily. His cleaning had prevented any comments about the state of her life. "Of course. So, curry?"

"Let's have a little sit down first, poppet." Her dad made himself comfortable on the sofa. Cactus immediately hopped up beside him. "So, tell us about this detective. Did he treat you well?"

It took every last ounce of strength for Motts to deal with the questions about Teo. Her parents moved from her one date to all the drama with Rose and Innis. She didn't know which was worse.

Both were equally awkward to chat about with her parents. Motts finally distracted them with curry. And even so, her mum still managed to draw the conversation around to Teo.

"And when are you seeing him again?"

Motts wanted to scream "never," if only to make the subject go away. "I don't know. He lives in Plymouth. His job is stressful and takes up large amounts of his time. I'll see him whenever he gets the chance to come and visit."

And hopefully, it will never be when you're here to humiliate me.

"What—"

"Is there anything for pudding?" her dad interjected. He winked at Motts when her mum immediately turned on him about his lack of manners. "I know, dear, but you love me despite all of my many faults."

"I have chocolate." Motts moved from the table into the kitchen. She lifted the container of treasure from her trip to the Kernow factory. "Don't think I have any other options for pudding."

"Why in the world do you have thirty bars of chocolate?" Her mum stared incredulously at the vast selection.

"Research." Motts shrugged. "How else will I know which flavour is my favourite? A thorough investigation is required. Besides, I'm not eating them all at the same time."

"I blame you." Her mum poked her dad in the side

and shook her head with a heavy sigh. "Of all our traits, you had to get your father's sweet tooth."

Her dad ignored the lecture, leaning forward to sift through the various flavours available. "Why don't we split one of the Bakewell Tart bars?"

They finished up dinner. Her parents eventually headed off to bed. She'd given them the larger bed and stayed on the futon herself.

Cactus leapt onto the bed, curling up on top of a pillow and watching Motts pace the room. She was too wound up to go to sleep. Her parents had thrown out her plans for the entire week.

Motts grabbed her laptop and moved onto the futon with Cactus. She dragged the blanket up to cover her. "What do you think the odds of them leaving before something else happens are?"

Meow.

"I agree." She dropped her head against the pillow. "It's going to be a disaster."

CHAPTER TWENTY

Innis had been released by the police. They'd had to, with no direct evidence aside from his own wife's assumptions. At least, that was the gossip Motts heard from Marnie early the next morning.

She'd fled the house before her parents woke up, leaving a note on the counter with her excuse of going to pick up breakfast for everyone. Her first stop had been to Griffin Brews, where she ran into Marnie chatting with Vina and Nish at the front counter. They immediately shared the news.

After delaying as long as possible, Motts grabbed a selection of pastries. She wandered outside the café, secured the box onto the basket, and got onto her bike. Her progress forward was halted when a vehicle swerved to park in front of her.

Bugger.

Innis stormed out of his van towards her. "You."

"Me?" Motts froze on her bicycle. She didn't know where to look, so she stared at his chin. It had a small scar hidden underneath the stubble. "I'm going home now."

"You need to quit interfering." He stepped closer to her.

Motts wrinkled her nose; he smelled like fish guts. "Your wife brought you to the attention of the police by throwing stones through my window."

"Innis. Shouldn't you be at your shop by now?" Nish strode out of the café. He came to a stop in front of Motts, making a barrier between her and the angry man. "And maybe you should quit trying to scare people."

"Fine." Innis's nostrils flared as he breathed heavily. After a moment, he stomped back to his van and drove away.

"You okay?" Nish wrapped an arm around her shoulders. "I'll chat with him later once he's cooled off."

"Not sure what good it'll do. I need to get home before my parents wake up." Motts's hands shook as she gripped the handlebars. She cycled unsteadily at first before getting herself under control. "Bye, Nish."

He yelled at her to be safe. Motts kept cycling. She cycled all the way to the base of the hill leading up to her cottage. As she came around the corner, Noel Watson skidded to a halt in front of her.

"Mr Watson." Motts managed to not say, "I presume." She kept thinking about Sherlock Holmes. "Were you up at the cottage?"

"What are you doing here?"

She blinked at him in confusion. "In Cornwall? On this street? In the universe? How existential are we talking?"

"You're in the way." He shoved by her, running down the street like she'd come down with a sudden case of fatal contagious viral infection. "Rude bint."

"Me?" Motts stared after him.

What had Noel been doing at the top of the hill? She hadn't seen him there before aside from when he'd been on the coastal path behind her cottage. *Should I mention this to Teo? I don't want to bother him.*

Motts trudged up the hill to the cottage, secured her bicycle next to the scooter, and made her way inside. She quietly muttered, "Hello."

Anyone?

Nope.

Well, thank goodness for small mercies.

Home alone except for my lovelies.

Sneaking through the cottage, Motts greeted Moss and offered her some breakfast. She left the extra coffees and pastries in the kitchen. Cactus followed her down the hall to the spare room.

"Success," Motts whispered. She curled back up under the blanket with her coffee, and Cactus nibbled at the edge of her pastry. "Bad kitty."

Meow.

"No, you can't have my breakfast." She put her headphones on to watch a YouTube video.

"Poppet?"

Motts groaned, shifting Cactus away and placing her coffee on the desk in the corner. She tripped over the duvet but finally made it to the door. "Dad?"

"Did something happen in the village?" Her dad had his phone in one hand and the coffee she'd left for him in the other. "Your uncle Tom sent me a text to check on you."

What's worse?

Village gossip, family gossip, or a combination of the two?

"Poppet?" her dad prompted as she got completely lost in thought over what was worse.

"Nothing happened." She dodged by him with Cactus on her heels. "Is Mum up as well?"

"Pineapple Mottley." He caught up to her in the kitchen. "What's going on?"

"Nothing." Motts didn't really have an answer for him. She didn't know how to explain the strange encounters she'd had with Noel and Innis. "Will you want a full English breakfast or are the pastries sufficient?"

Her dad simply stared at her until she stopped fussing with the bag from Griffin Brews. "Talk to me."

She leaned against the counter with a sigh of resignation. "I can't answer your question. I don't know what's happening. Until the police make an arrest, I'm not sure anyone will have answers."

"Have we complicated your life by coming down again?" He chuckled when she turned away to fuss with Cactus's breakfast. "We weren't expecting to be empty nesters."

"Ever?" Motts didn't think even in London that she'd have been happy to live with her parents for the rest of her life. She'd wanted to spread her wings a little for years, even if she'd been later than most people. "Are you going to visit every month?"

"You could be less horrified by the concept." He sipped his coffee, then leaned back to glance down the hallway. "Your mum went into the bedroom. How about we fix up some easy eggs and toast to go with your pastries?"

She loved her parents.

She genuinely adored them. She did.

By the end of the first day of their visit, Motts had reached the end of her tether. Her dad was brilliant. He didn't press her for anything but was content to simply spend time together.

Her mum wanted to solve all of her problems—particularly the ones she imagined Motts had. They'd butted heads already over the way the garden had been situated. Her main gripe had been over Motts refusing to introduce to them to Teo.

The next morning, Motts fled the cottage after her mum decided to reorganise the kitchen. *It's not logical, darling. We'll set it up so you don't have to stress over where the mugs and tea are.*

Deciding not to scream in frustration, Motts grabbed her scooter and rode down to the village in the pouring rain. She parked under the awning in front of Griffin Brews. Vina simply raised her eyebrows when Motts threw herself down onto her favourite chair in the corner and rested her head against the table.

"Rough morning?"

"Mum has gone from critiquing my garden to shuffling around everything in my kitchen cabinets." Motts turned her head slightly to see Vina, who crouched next to the table. "I'm dripping on the floor."

"Driving through a spring shower will do that to you. Let me grab a towel. Nish can fix you up with a warm mug of chocolate chai." Vina patted her on the shoulder. "Don't worry about your cabinet. We can rearrange everything when they leave. You might even decide to declutter."

Motts narrowed her eyes on her. "Declutter."

"It's not a dirty word."

"You fell into the organising cult on YouTube, didn't you?" Motts gratefully accepted the small tea towel Nish tossed at her. She wiped her arms and face off, then tried to dry her hair a little. "I don't own enough to declutter."

"Fair enough." Vina headed off into the kitchen, likely to grab a larger towel.

"Here you go, Motts." Nish had returned with a mug and set it on the table. "Want a pie, cake, sandwich? Amma whipped up a fresh batch of spiced fruit pies. They're cooling in the kitchen. She won't mind my nicking one for you."

"I could eat." Motts would never turn down one of

Leena's creations. She worked magic with spice, whether sweet or savoury. "Can I hide here forever?"

"They do know where the café is, Mottsy." Vina wrapped a large towel around her shoulders. She grabbed the small tea towel and used it to clean up the puddle under the chair. "Want to borrow a spare set of clothes? I've got a bag in the office with jeans and a button-up. They should fit you fine—maybe a smidge too big given our height difference."

"We're not the same size on any set of measurements. I'll dry off eventually." Motts wasn't overly concerned. "Pie?"

"Mottsy—"

Nish elbowed his sister in the side, cutting her off. "Amma's calling you."

"She's not. I can't hear her, and my hearing is better than both of yours," Motts pointed out.

Nish pinched the bridge of his nose while Vina laughed at him. "Are they still wanting to meet Teo?"

Motts had the strangest feeling she'd missed something. It wasn't the first time and wouldn't be the last. "Of course they do. I haven't been out with someone since Vina and I split. They're not interested in how it was more of a friend thing than a full-on date."

"Parents," Nish sympathised. "Oh, a customer. Be back."

Vina slipped into the chair across from her. "It's pouring down rain out there."

"Yes, I'm aware." Motts squeezed water out of her hair into the towel.

"You can't ride home until it stops. Why don't you sneak upstairs with me? We've got the apartment all kitted out for late night baking. Have a hot shower. Change into some dry clothes. If you won't wear mine, I'll run across the street to pick up something from the charity shop in your size." Vina pushed the mug of warm tea closer to her. "You'll catch a cold if you sit in those clothes to dry."

"I'm fine."

"No, you're overwhelmed by your parents and everything else. Have a long, hot shower. If nothing else, it'll warm you up and stop you from shivering." Vina got to her feet and came around the table to try to lift Motts up. "Please?"

"Fine."

They wandered through the kitchen to the narrow stairs leading up to the upstairs apartment. Vina ran the shower and set out a towel for her. She ushered Motts into the bathroom, leaving her with the instruction to take her time.

"I do know how to bathe myself," Motts grumbled.

"I'll run over to the shop to grab some clothes for

you. Or I'll drive up to the cottage to grab a spare set of yours so you can't complain about my spending money unnecessarily." Vina was gone before Motts could argue.

Well, nothing to do but shower since the water's already running.

Why is everyone so pushy all of a sudden?

It's infuriating.

It was late in the afternoon when Motts finally returned home to the cottage. Her mum had definitely been cooking. She could smell sausage and knew her mum had made toad-in-the-hole for dinner.

Food was definitely the way to Motts's heart after a tension-filled day. She found her parents deep in conversation in the kitchen. They both smiled when she stepped hesitantly closer.

"Toad-in-the-hole?"

"Thought you might enjoy a home-cooked meal." Her mum gestured to the baking pan cooling on the counter. "Are you ready for a bite? Or is it too early?"

"It's fine." Motts hated the stilted conversation. She wished her mum didn't always take things so personally. It wasn't an attack if she wanted to keep her cottage different than her childhood home had been. Growing up meant figuring out things on her own. "Thanks, Mum."

Please let them go home soon.

I might barricade myself in the spare room if they don't.

Her parents left early the next morning. There had been no heart-to-heart conversations. Motts supposed they'd always see her as their little girl, even if it annoyed her to no end.

After spending half the morning returning her mugs to their rightful home, Motts tried to get into the groove of her normal day. She messed up six paper tulips and almost ruined one of her quilling projects. Her mind was clearly telling her to get out of the cottage.

The skies had cleared late in the previous evening. Motts wandered out into the garden with Cactus on his leash. They both enjoyed the breeze coming in off the sea with the bright sun overhead.

Her herb patch was doing well with the rain and sun. She had high hopes it would begin to sprout in the next month or two. New growth in what had been a scene of a tragedy.

It was almost poetic.

"Your garden's doing well."

Motts tightened her fingers on the leash. She hadn't heard anyone walking down the path along her fence. "Yes."

Noel leaned against the fence casually. "Are you recovered from your accident?"

"My accident?"

"Heard you'd been run over."

She didn't know how to respond to his statement. It wasn't a question. "Not really an accident if someone runs you over, is it?"

The odd encounter became even stranger when he simply walked down the path. Where was he going? He lived (and worked) in the opposite direction. Why did he keep heading down the coastal path by her cottage?

What was down there?

The question ate at her all morning. Motts found curiosity once again driving her to explore where she probably shouldn't. She locked up the cottage and headed off the path in the direction Noel had gone earlier in the day.

Despite walking for over an hour, Motts never discovered anything of particular interest. She turned around, retracing her steps to avoid being stuck out in the dark on the rocky path. Cactus waited anxiously for her, his little face almost pressed against the glass of the back window.

Meow.

Motts bent down to lift him up when she got

inside the cottage. "Did you miss me? I was gone longer than I intended, wasn't I?"

Deciding to warm up with a mug of tea, Motts got the kettle going. She set a bowl of treats out for Cactus, who acted as though he hadn't been fed in three weeks. He purred between bites of food.

"At least we have the cottage to ourselves again."

CHAPTER TWENTY-ONE

Spring continued to roll through March. Motts, despite her allergies, found herself excited for later in the season and going into summer. She knew from holidays as a child how beautiful Polperro was.

She didn't have the same enthusiasm for the tourists who would descend on the village. It was the one downside to Cornwall. River and Nish had both told her not to borrow trouble; Vina had laughed at them, knowing how much Motts panicked over things far off in the future.

They'd been over every night since her parents left. At the end of the week, though, River and Nish were taking a brief holiday together. Vina and her new girlfriend had gone off to London for a three-day weekend.

Motts intended to settle in for the weekend. She wanted to finish up her quilled sari project for Leena. A few days focused on it would likely get her where she wanted.

A knock on the door interrupted her in the middle of finishing breakfast. She put her plate in the microwave to keep Cactus from filching from her food. Her heart dropped into her stomach when she opened the door to find Innis preparing to knock a second time.

"I want to talk."

Motts wondered if he'd planned this conversation around a time when her friends were all away from the village. She gripped the doorknob tightly. It was tempting to slam the door. "Why? You've shouted quite a lot at me over the last few weeks. What else could you have to say?"

"I brought a sultana cake from Rose. She thought we might apologise for the rough welcome to the village." Innis thrust the package at her. "It's not poisoned."

Well, I certainly feel reassured.

"Thanks?" Motts took the package and held it gingerly. She planned to throw the cake away the second Innis left. "Is that all you wanted to say?"

"Can I come in?"

"No." Motts didn't trust the man enough to be in the cottage alone with him. "Sorry."

Innis broke into a smile that made him seem less menacing. "I deserve the mistrust. Why don't we sit on the bench?"

After a second of consideration, Motts found, once again, her curiosity got the better of her. She stepped outside, closing the door behind her. Innis sat on the bench and thankfully didn't comment when she remained standing close by.

"My sister and I...." Innis trailed off. He breathed in deeply before trying again. "Rhona wanted a lifestyle Polperro and the fish shop couldn't offer her. She wanted romance, London, and everything young people seem to cling to as a measure of success and happiness."

"And you disagreed?" Motts prompted when he fell silent.

"I worried." He bent forward with his elbows on his knees. "Rose says I turned into my da after he passed. Who knows. Rhona never told me about the sale. We didn't talk. We were stubborn. But I never hurt my sister. I didn't want her around those boys."

"Those boys?" Motts found herself drawn into the conversation. "You mean Danny?"

"Him. And his friends. They chased after her.

Never trusted them. Even now, why haven't they picked up Danny?" Innis slapped his hand against his leg in obvious frustration. "And the Watson lad. After Rhona's disappearance, we eventually cleared out some of her things. Rose donated them to the charity shop."

Motts nodded, waiting for him to explain the significance.

"A week or two after, I spotted him wearing one of her scarves. He still wears it in the winter." Innis smacked his leg a second time. "I wanted to rip it off his neck."

Better than strangling him with it.

"Maybe he liked her." Motts did honestly find Noel's behaviour a little strange. "Did he ever date Rhona?"

"Never. I'm not sure she liked him very much, even as a friend." Innis got to his feet, and Motts took a step back. "I am sorry. You haven't seen us at our best."

"Did Rose run me over?" Motts decided to press the question, wanting to see how he'd respond.

"My Rose? Never," Innis denied vehemently. "She threw the rock, yes, but she'd never want to cause physical harm to someone."

And strangely enough, Motts believed him. She said goodbye and returned to the cottage. The talk had left her wondering who had been involved in Rhona's death.

Did she believe Innis wasn't involved? Maybe. She thought he might be capable of accidentally killing his sister in the middle of an argument.

Had he protested too much?

Heading out into her garden, Motts walked Cactus before returning to the cottage. She resisted the temptation to head down to the village. Noel hadn't exactly been welcoming the few times she'd met him.

Odd. Angry. But not welcoming.

After wasting over an hour trying to make progress on her quilling masterpiece, Motts gave up the ruse. She dithered between going on her own or finding someone to be nosy with her. She eventually sent a text to Teo.

A good and bad idea.

Brilliant because Motts had missed him over the last few days, particularly when she cracked open a bar of chocolate. Teo turned out to be in Looe visiting his parents; he wondered if she wanted to go out for supper.

She agreed. And immediately regretted her decision. Not going to dinner with Teo; she'd enjoyed spending time with him before. But she wasn't eagerly anticipating visiting a busy restaurant.

As Motts had already said yes, she didn't feel comfortable backing out. By the time Teo arrived to pick her up, she'd managed to stress herself out to the point of being sick. He seemed surprised to see her so frazzled.

"What's wrong?" Teo strode forward to take her hand gently. "We don't have to go out."

"I had a panic attack." Motts pulled her hand away, twisting her fingers together anxiously. "I kept thinking about crowded restaurants and embarrassing myself."

"Polperro's not really known for takeaway." Teo followed her into the cottage, where she immediately curled up on the sofa with Cactus beside her. "Unless you want fish and chips. Griffin Brews is closed for the weekend. How about I make a quick trip back to Looe, grab a pizza or something greasy and comforting. We can chill here for dinner instead of stressing you out further by going to some restaurant."

"You don't mind the drive?"

"I've done more driving than the twenty minutes or so it'll take me to get there and back. I know the perfect place for a takeaway; a friend of mine runs the place." Teo gave Cactus's head a pat. "Any specific cravings?"

Motts shook her head. "I hate being a bother."

"You're not a bother. My friend's inquiring questions about who my date is will *definitely* be more of an annoyance than you could ever be. I'll even get a little something special for Cactus," Teo promised.

She watched him leave and forced herself to get up and lock the door. Cactus followed her down the hall. "I think I like him."

Meow.

"Yes, he's very considerate to get you a treat. Smart man." Motts stayed on the couch and waited for his return. She greatly appreciated Teo's kindness to her. "We'll have to keep him around."

Turning on one of her favourite vlogger channels, Motts allowed the stress to slowly bleed away. When Teo returned, her anxiety had dropped significantly. She felt capable of holding a conversation with him.

"He made tapas for us. Croatian-Cornish-inspired tapas." Teo held up two bags filled with small containers. "I said I was bringing dinner for a date, and this is what he gave me."

Motts tried not to laugh at how disgruntled he appeared. "They'll be lovely."

"I'm going to tell his mother." Teo had a slightly vicious smile on his face. Motts imagined he appeared the same way when a criminal confessed under interrogation. "She goes to my knitting club."

"Right, knitting. What's your current project?"

Teo shifted both of the bags into one hand and grabbed his phone out of his pocket. He scrolled through before twisting the screen around to show a greyish blue knitted lace circle. "I haven't done much yet. It'll be a shawl eventually, but it's the most complicated pattern I've attempted."

Over the course of their meal of various dishes, Motts told him about her conversation with Innis. Teo agreed with her that his comments on Danny and Noel were interesting. He did say they were continuing to investigate the small group of friends who'd hung around Rhona.

"Why would he wear her scarf?"

"Unrequited love?" Teo speared a piece of Komiška pogača. He'd described the dish as a savoury pie. It reminded Motts of a beautifully flavoured combination of a tomato pie and a salty onion focaccia. "Maybe he lost Rhona to Danny?"

"She was a person, not a prize," Motts muttered.

"I agree." He held up his hands in surrender. "It's something we have to consider."

"Do you know what vehicles Noel owns or has access to?" Motts had come to the conclusion that her accident and the discovery of Rhona's body had to be connected. "I don't believe Rose attacked me."

"Aside from throwing a rock through your window? And possibly locking you in the shed?"

Motts glared at him but had to laugh when he simply grinned. She liked the way he smiled at her. "Did she admit to locking me in the shed?"

"No."

"There you go then."

"Yes, because criminals never lie to the police." Teo waved his fork, sending a crumb flying. He laughed when Cactus tried to pounce immediately on the piece of pie. "Though, I agree with you. I don't believe Rose did anything aside from breaking your window."

"So, who did run me over?"

"I wish you'd stop saying it so casually." His hand clenched around the fork. "But to answer your question, I'm not sure yet. We're still trying to track down who stole the vehicle involved."

"Okay." Motts let the subject go. She had a feeling Teo knew more but he couldn't or wouldn't share with her yet. "Want to visit the charity shop with me?"

Teo set his fork down. "No. I'll have Inspector Ash follow up with Noel. He knows him better. If I go, he's already going to be on edge."

"I could—"

"Stay away from anyone who might potentially have committed murder," he said firmly.

Motts wasn't sold on Noel being the killer, but she saw the wisdom in not putting herself in danger. "I wasn't trying to be around them when they ran me over."

"Try your best." Teo set his plate on the coffee table. He moved around to sit next to her on the couch. "One thing I've learnt since this cold case landed on my desk is that quite a lot of people care about your well-being. And I include myself in that group. You matter."

Motts shifted uneasily on the sofa. She never knew how to handle emotional moments. "I promise to try not to run headfirst into any other vehicles."

Teo was surprised into a laugh. "Good enough."

CHAPTER TWENTY-TWO

"Did you kiss?"

Motts stared at Vina. Her best friend had come over early in the morning when she'd gotten back into town. She'd brought coffee and doughnuts, so Motts was prepared to forgive her for waking her. "I know it's hard for you to grasp, but not everyone wants physical contact beyond holding hands and hugging."

"So, no snogs on the sofa with Cactus watching?" Vina dodged away from Motts, who swatted at her. "I'll stop. I'm only teasing."

"Doubtful." Motts grabbed another doughnut. "My parents haven't called me since they left. Not even Dad."

"Maybe your uncle's chat convinced them to give you time to settle?"

"Maybe." Motts hoped they hadn't gotten their feelings hurt. She was torn between wanting space and not wanting to ruin her relationship with them. "I hope it's something that simple."

Over their quick sugary breakfast, Vina told her all about her long weekend away with her girlfriend. Motts, in return, shared her intriguing chat with Innis. She hadn't had much to say about her brief supper with Teo.

"We could always have a sneaky chat with Noel at the charity shop." Vina finished up the last dregs of her coffee. "It's on my way to the café. Or, maybe we should see what Danny Orchard has to say about all of this. If they were all friends, he might have noticed his friend's puppy love."

"And we know Danny isn't a killer, so Teo can't be upset." Motts gathered up the remnants of their breakfast and put the dishes in the sink. She dropped the rubbish in the bin. "Can you feed Moss and Cactus while I change into something that isn't pyjamas?"

With her beloved pets taken care of, Motts dashed into her bedroom. She swapped her comfortable pyjamas for jeans and an oversized jumper. Vina was having a whispered conversation with Moss when she returned to the living room.

"Stop chatting up my turtle." Motts adjusted her

jumper, pulling the sleeves down to where they covered her fingers almost completely. "I'll follow you down to Danny's."

"I do know how to drive, Mottsy," Vina complained.

"I'm aware, but you need to get to work, and I have errands to run." Motts grabbed her helmet from the nearby side table. "Did you feed my babies?"

"Of course." Vina followed her out of the cottage. "Are you sure you don't want to run by the charity shop?"

With a shake of her head, Motts wheeled her scooter out. She didn't want to approach Noel until she had a better understanding of what had happened before Rhona's death. Innis clearly didn't know, and neither did Rose, so the only other person she could ask was Danny.

Following Vina in her car, Motts had a sinking suspicion Danny might be reticent to talk with them. She also had a feeling Teo wouldn't approve of her continuing to investigate. Her curiosity kept her from simply letting it go.

She couldn't.

Every time Motts thought about Rhona, her old school friend Jenny came to mind as well. She'd never gotten answers for Jenny. And her heart broke at the idea of the same thing happening once again.

They barely parked before Danny came rushing out towards them. He grabbed them by the arms and dragged them around the corner out of the view of the shop. Vina exchanged a bewildered glance with Motts.

"Danny?" Motts wrenched her arm out of his grasp. "What the devil is going on?"

"I don't want my granddad to see you. He doesn't approve." Danny pressed his lips together. He glared at the two of them. "You don't want flowers."

"We might," Vina retorted.

"You don't." He gestured wildly, narrowly missing hitting her. "What do you want now?"

"Can we ask you another question about Noel?" Motts drew back at the outraged light in his eyes. "Just one."

Danny shook his head and stormed off a few steps, muttering to himself. He breathed deeply several times before finally returning. "Ask your questions."

Motts stared at him. He exuded an intense, angry vibe that made her want to draw into her shell like Moss often did. "I...."

"Did Noel fancy Rhona?" Vina asked when she realised Motts was struggling. "Was there a love triangle going on?"

"No." Danny peered beyond them. "She didn't like him."

"She didn't have to." Motts listened to enough true crime podcasts to know women were frequently murdered in similar situations. "Did you ever see him acting jealous of your relationship?"

"How would I know?" Danny kept glancing behind them towards the corner. "I've got to go. My granddad will be waiting for me. Why don't you both mind your own business on this one, yeah?"

Motts watched him stomp off away from them. She remembered her first confrontation with Danny's grandfather. He'd been angry about her digging in the garden. "I wonder if we're questioning the wrong member of the Orchard family."

"Not sure any member of the family would be eager to talk to us." Vina looped her arm around Motts and guided her down the pavement toward where they'd parked their vehicles. "His reaction to his grandfather seeing him answering questions about Rhona is odd."

"Suspicious."

"That too." She pulled her keys out of her pocket. "Want to come hang out at the café?"

Motts waved off the invitation with a smile. "I'll visit you later."

Vina narrowed her eyes. "Mottsy."

"Yes?"

"Be careful, alright?" She opened her mouth to say something but seemed to reconsider. "I'll text you in the afternoon to see if you're interested in having supper."

After watching Vina drive off, Motts considered her options. She knew trying to talk to either Danny or his grandfather would likely end up in a shouting match. At best. If the elder Orchard was involved, yelling might be the least of her problems.

Riding her scooter back up the hill, Motts wandered into her cottage, lost in thought. She flopped on the couch and cuddled Cactus absently. In all the fuss, she'd actually forgotten about the elder Orchard.

Could he have killed Rhona? Why? Motts honestly had no idea what would've driven him.

Meow.

"No, I don't know why anyone would want to kill her." She hefted Cactus up to curl up in the crook of her neck while she rested against the sofa cushion. "Murder makes no sense."

Cactus gave a more insistent meow, butting his head against her chin. Motts followed his gaze over to the bowl Vina had set out for him. She'd put some of his snacks instead of his food inside.

"Did Auntie Vina give you the wrong food?" Motts dragged herself off the couch with Cactus still held in her arms. She grabbed the dish from the windowsill. "What a clever kitten you are."

The question of Rhona's death continued to plague her mind throughout the day. They'd likely never know how she died unless the killer confessed. She knew Teo suspected poison, given the foxglove in the box.

Dried flower petals in a buried tin in the garden didn't really amount to a smoking gun. They could've been put there for sentimental reasons. And if they were the cause of Rhona's death, how had she ingested them?

"Was Danny's grandfather trying to protect his grandson or their family name? Or did Innis kill his sister to keep the Salty Seaman from being sold?" Motts tapped her finger against the side of the bag of cat food while thinking. "Or did Noel harbour jealousy in his heart? If he couldn't be with Rhona, then no one else could?"

Cactus, unfortunately, didn't have any answers for her. He tried his best. His purring was comforting, though.

After an entire afternoon and evening considering, Motts text messaged Teo about the odd conversation with Danny. She also told him about the confrontation with the elder Mr Orchard right before Rhona had been found in the garden. He thanked her but sternly asked her to stay away from the family.

And she intended to keep her distance.

Motts spent her morning answering emails, starting two new flower bouquets for Marnie's shop, and walking with Cactus in the garden. He enjoyed his forays outside. She watched him chasing after butterflies for a while.

"Are you in the garden?"

Motts immediately lifted Cactus into her arms. She went over to the garden gate and found a worried Constable Stone. "I am in the garden."

He smiled, though she thought his usually broad grin seemed strained. "Detective Inspector Herceg asked me to check in on you. He and Perry went to speak with Innis, but Rose claims not to know where he went. They decided to follow up with Danny and his granddad after your encounter. Mr Orchard threw a punch, so he's been brought to Plymouth for questioning."

"He threw a punch? He's in his seventies." Motts rested her chin on Cactus's head, allowing his purring to comfort her. "I thought he was grumpy but not violent."

Hughie shrugged. "DI Herceg wanted you to stay close to home until they've followed up with Innis."

"Is he the killer then?" Motts had put Innis on the bottom of her list of suspects. She didn't honestly think him capable. Then again, they didn't know how Rhona died; it might've been an accident. Innis was *definitely* capable of an act of impulsive violence. "Are they sure?"

"You know I'd tell you if I could. They only want to talk to him." Hughie reached out to rub Cactus's ear. "You call me if you need anything at all, alright? Even if you think it's a bother, you pick up the phone."

"I will," Motts promised.

"Right. I'm on my way to revisit the Salty Seaman. Rose might be more amenable to chatting with me. The inspectors are an intimidatingly solemn duo when they want to be." He smiled at her. "Try not to worry too much."

Motts waved at him and watched him trot down the path to his vehicle. She carried Cactus inside and set him on the counter to get some water. "What do you think? Is it Innis or Mr Orchard?"

Meow.

"I don't know either. I don't want to believe it's Innis, not after our conversation the other day." She filled the kettle with water and turned it on. A cup of her favourite hot chocolate would be the perfect balm to her sudden onset of anxiety. She grabbed one of her many turtle mugs—this one had a baby sea turtle on one side with "it's been a shell of a day" on the other. River had gotten it for her birthday a few years prior. "It's going to be fine."

Meow.

"Yes, I need to practise so I sound like I believe myself." Motts tried not to stress about things she had no control over. She really did. "I'm going to be fine."

The more I say it, the less I believe it.

Is that how positive affirmations are supposed to work?

Probably not.

Meow.

"Yes, I hear the kettle whistling." Motts poured the water into her mug and stirred the hot chocolate. "I'll be fine. Fine finicky festers ferociously. Fine."

CHAPTER TWENTY-THREE

Midway through the day, Motts heard her phone beeping. She scrambled out of the spare room, trying to find her mobile. It wasn't in her pockets or in the pockets of any of her hoodies and coats, and eventually she found it stuffed between the cushions of her sofa.

Who is texting me?

She didn't immediately recognise the number. It didn't belong to any of her friends or family. She sent a message back asking the person to identify themselves.

Why is Danny Orchard texting me?

In his message, Danny claimed to want to meet up with her. She wondered if his granddad's arrest had given him the courage to speak. He wanted to meet in private to avoid anyone in the village knowing.

Hughie had asked her to stay in the cottage. The coastal path was technically behind her cottage. And it definitely offered more privacy than arguing on the street outside the Orchard nursery.

There was a long pause between her message and a reply. Danny agreed to meet up with her in an hour down the path. There was a small trail off The Warren leading down to the cliff and a Spy House lighthouse that tourists loved to photograph; Motts had walked it a few times herself.

"Is this a bad idea?" Motts glanced up at Cactus, who sat on the back of the sofa, watching her pulling on her walking boots. "Hughie did say to stay home. But what if Danny wants to confess that his granddad murdered Rhona? I could solve the case."

Meow.

"Alright, fine. I'll send Teo a text." Motts could've called him or Hughie, but the idea of talking on the phone only added more stress to the situation. "He might have some advice for what to ask Danny."

With her text sent, Motts decided to get a head start down the path. She enjoyed walking. The fresh air off the sea might help clear her mind.

It didn't.

Her anxiety levels continued to rise. *Maybe I should've waited to hear from Teo?* She'd checked her phone every few seconds, but nothing. If he were interrogating Mr Orchard, perhaps he'd left his phone in the office.

Any knowledge Motts had of police procedure came from podcasts and YouTube videos on true crime. She didn't think they always got things right. Would Teo keep his phone on him while questioning someone?

Checking her phone for the tenth time, Motts found a text from Danny saying he'd be a little late. *Brilliant, more time to stress.* She finally reached the lighthouse. The day had turned grey and blustery, so she had the viewing spot all to herself.

She sat on one of the steps leading down beyond the lighthouse and tucked her hands into her pockets. Her fingers gripped the phone in her pocket. Heading home began to sound like an incredibly brilliant idea.

Why did I agree to this?

And why didn't I put on my coat or a thick jumper instead of this hoodie?

Motts pulled her mobile out of her pocket when it rang. She answered on the fourth ring. "Teo?"

"What *are* you doing?" He sounded angry, but his voice kept cutting out.

Motts walked up the steps a little way. "I can't hear you. It's really windy. What's happened?"

"Go... Orchard... almost there... hello?"

Motts pulled her phone away from her ear when they were disconnected. She tried to call him back, but the signal wouldn't go through. "Bugger."

Pacing back and forth for several minutes, Motts decided she'd made a massive mistake. Danny could come by her cottage if he wanted a chat. She shoved her phone into her pocket and turned to head home.

"Noel." She found herself not completely surprised to see him.

"Hello." Noel Watson stood on the steps above her. She hadn't heard him approach with the wind coming off the sea. "Danny couldn't make it. He lent me his phone."

"Oh?" Motts didn't quite believe him and wondered if Danny had been hurt. She stumbled back down the steps until she was leaning against the lighthouse. "Why would he lend you his mobile? I don't even like people touching mine."

Okay, that's not the point to be worried about.

Why is he looming over me?

Why did I agree to meet Danny?

Noel held the phone out, pointing it at Motts like a weapon. "Danny told me all about your questions. He demanded to know if I'd hurt Rhona. If I'd been jealous. Jealous. What a load of absolute rubbish. Me?

Jealous of him. He's done nothing with his life but work for his family."

"You run your family's charity shop."

"Shut the bloody hell up." Noel jabbed the phone into her shoulder. "He didn't deserve her."

Motts shifted further to the side, trying to keep her footing on the slick steps. It had started to drizzle, which did nothing to stop her shivering from cold and fear. "And you deserved Rhona?"

"I had plans and dreams. Danny only wanted to dig around in the dirt with plants." Noel sneered. He still held the phone tightly, waving it around while he shouted. "She could've had *me*."

"Could she?" Motts didn't know what the right way was to calm the situation. Noel had definitely gone beyond the point of being reasoned with. He seemed content to throw a temper tantrum. "Rhona loved Danny."

"He didn't deserve her," Noel reiterated. He slammed Danny's phone against the ground. It bounced down the steps, past the railing and down toward the sea. She definitely had no intentions of following its path. "I told her I loved her."

"And how did Rhona feel about you?" She wanted to draw out the conversation. One, because she wanted answers, but also in the hopes someone would come along and notice them. "Was she in love with you?"

Her questions sent Noel off on another tangent. He ranted about Rhona turning him down. Motts tried to edge away from him, out of reach, while he called the woman he claimed to love vile names.

Cursing her curiosity, Motts watched Noel warily. He hadn't worn himself out yet. She wondered how everyone had missed his obvious stalker tendencies towards Rhona.

He went on and on about how he'd followed Rhona and Danny on their dates. He even tried to warn Innis and Rose. Motts wondered if the young woman had had any inclination she was being tracked around the small village so closely.

"She wouldn't listen." Noel stepped closer to her. "I warned her. I told her Danny would only drag her down."

Motts cringed away from him. His breath washed across her, and he'd definitely had a few pints before tricking her into meeting. "What happened to Rhona?"

"She loved chocolates."

Motts tilted her head in confusion. *Chocolates? What?* "Did she?"

"She did." Noel's smile wasn't anywhere near as

friendly as Hughie's or as unique as Teo's. His felt menacing and terrifying. "My mum makes chocolate truffles. I added a special ingredient. Crushed up the seeds myself. Saved the petals, had to put them in my little memory box as a memento of our special time together."

Their special time together.

"Foxglove." She knew the flowers in the tin had been connected to Rhona's death. "The dried petals."

"Picked them straight from the Orchards's garden." Noel seemed pleased with his cleverness. "She chose him. Him. Over me. She never appreciated my worth. My intelligence."

Jealousy did strange things to people. Motts remembered her dad once talking about how envy and possessiveness could poison any relationship. She'd never seen it manifested so violently in person.

Then again, how many true crime podcasts had she listened to where the killer in a case had been driven by jealousy?

"I wanted the cottage to be mine."

Motts's head snapped around toward Noel in surprise. "What?"

"I could've bought the cottage if you hadn't decided to move in." Noel clearly didn't know her family well; River would've taken the home if Motts hadn't. "She wouldn't be able to tell me to go away then."

Right.

His angry confession made her wonder, though. Had Noel been the one to try to run her over? Maybe it hadn't been a warning but an attempt on her life.

"You drove into me," she accused.

Noel sneered at her. "I missed."

"Not from my perspective." Motts mentally berated herself. She didn't need to antagonise him. It wouldn't keep her alive. "Was the bracelet yours? Why bury the tin in the garden? Why not keep it with you?"

While Noel proceeded to brag about his own brilliance, Motts glanced around, trying to figure out how to get away from him. She had no intentions of letting him attack, if that was the plan. He stalked back and forth on the step in front of her, creating a physical block in the path.

I will get out of this.

Someone has to take care of Cactus and Moss.

"You're not listening," Noel complained. He stomped his foot like a toddler having a temper tantrum over a broken toy. "You're just like her."

"Not really." Motts dodged out of the way when he lunged for her. They slipped on the rain-slicked steps. Her head smacked against the side of the lighthouse, and her vision blurred slightly. "Bugger."

"Why couldn't you mind your own business? You had to dig around in the garden." Noel struggled to get to his feet. He kicked out at her, and Motts rolled out of the way of his foot. "You nosy cow."

"You left a body in my garden. And I refuse to have another unsolved mystery on my conscience." Motts scrambled for purchase on the steps. She kept slipping closer to the railing and the edge of the cliff beyond. She caught her foot on a pole and saved herself from going further down. "It didn't take a genius to figure out who did it."

Technically, I didn't figure it out.

He doesn't need to know.

"I won't leave a body this time." Noel managed to get to his feet and started towards her. "You'll be another tragic case of a tourist getting too close to the edge of a cliff. Happens all the time."

I am not going over the edge of a cliff.

I'm not.

There was no purchase for her hands in the ground around the lighthouse. Noel loomed over her, trying to shove her with his foot. He bent to push with his hands when that failed.

Motts slipped closer to the edge, her feet dangling

off it. She gripped tightly to the safety railing. "Listen, you absolute berk. I am *not* going off this cliff. It's not happening."

Noel kept trying to peel her fingers away from the pole. "Let go."

"No." Motts wanted to laugh at the absurdity of the surreal aspect of the moment. Did he genuinely believe she'd just voluntarily slide over the edge? She wanted to scream for help, but who'd hear her? "Will you stop it?"

Noel ignored her. He managed to remove one of her hands from the pole. She slipped further down. "Rhona died so much easier. Why won't you cooperate?"

"Berk." She didn't get a chance to say anything else. Noel suddenly disappeared from her view. "I should've stayed in bed."

Terrifying moments in life, Motts decided, happened both insanely fast and in slow motion. She'd been dangling halfway down an incline toward the edge of a cliff one second, then was yanked up to safety in the next instant. Teo crushed her in his arms, twisting her away from the view of Constable Stone and Inspector Ash, who'd wrestled Noel to the ground.

"You didn't say freeze. Police always say freeze." Motts trembled in his arms. She was drenched to the bone, but her shivering had nothing to do with the chill and damp from the rain. "Freezing felons fancy frolicking."

"We're not on some show on the telly." Teo laughed, though it sounded a little strained. "Let's get you to the hospital."

"I'm fine."

"Your head is bleeding." He carried her quickly up the stairs, around Noel and the police pinning him to the ground. "Let's get you out of here."

CHAPTER TWENTY-FOUR

Despite Teo's urging, Motts had insisted on going to the small local clinic. She felt a little sore but nothing worse. The bleeding on her head from hitting the lighthouse had stopped, so to her mind, there was no point in making a dramatic trip to the hospital.

The doctor checked her over, gave her some paracetamol, and sent her home to rest. Teo drove from the clinic to the cottage in silence. His hands gripped the steering wheel so tightly, Motts worried he might break it or hurt his fingers.

Teo parked outside the cottage behind the two cars already there. He twisted around in the seat slightly to face her. "I'll take your statement later. Why don't we get you inside? You'll want to change into dry clothes."

He sounded so calm. Motts didn't know how to

respond to the suddenly professional police officer sitting beside her. She wondered if he was as shell-shocked as she felt; maybe falling back on his training kept him going.

Motts nodded shakily and got out of the vehicle. Her legs almost went out from under her; she rested her hand against the car to regain her balance. "I just need a minute."

Teo moved quickly over to her side. He wrapped his arm around her. "Can I help?"

"Maybe we should go to the hospital." Motts leaned into his support. "We could drive."

"You can't avoid the crowd in your cottage forever." Teo didn't appear to have any sympathy for her. "When my call disconnected, I immediately reached out to Constable Stone. He assured me that you'd promised to stay in the cottage. He, in turn, called your cousin to see if he'd seen you. We all converged on your cottage as quickly as possible."

Motts started to struggle to process what he was saying. "Right."

After the adrenaline had faded away, Motts simply felt exhausted and cold. She knew the doctor had suggested warming up. Teo seemed to sense her flagging energy and carried her the rest of the way to the cottage.

Vina came out of the front door with Nish and River close behind. "Mottsy."

"I'm fine," Motts promised.

"You're not, but you will be." Teo eased between the trio to get Motts into the cottage. He glanced back at Vina. "Maybe you could help her to her room?"

There was a bit of grumbling between the group gathered in her living room. Motts tuned out all of it. She barely noticed Vina easing her arm around Motts's shoulders to guide her down toward her bedroom.

"We'll sort you out, won't we?" Vina paused to let Cactus into the room. "I swear, he knew something was wrong. As soon as River let us into the cottage, he tried to get us to go outside. We had to lift him up and hold him."

In the sanctity of her bedroom with Cactus and Vina, Motts collapsed on her bed. Her hands continued to shake, no matter what she did. They clutched as though still clinging to the railing for life; she had blisters on a few of her fingers from the effort as a reminder.

"Nish is so much better at calm and collected. I do the panicky helter-skelter." Vina knelt in front of her, resting her hands on Motts's wet jeans. "I'll run the water for you. A lovely hot bath will do you the world of good. Amma was cooking up a storm when we left.

You know she believes her food can cure any number of illnesses."

"It can," Motts muttered through chattering teeth. "How can I lounge in the bath with all those people in the living room?"

"All those people love and care about you." Vina tapped her on the nose gently. "Even Teo. I'm convinced he's going to be head-over-heels for you. They'll all wait until you're warm and in your comfy clothes."

"Okay."

"I am the all-knowing Vina. You should listen to me," she teased. "Right. I'll check on the bath. I put your favourite sudsy stuff in the water already. You strip down to your pants."

"Vina."

She laughed at Motts's outraged glare. "Fine. You go in and check on the bath. I'll dig through your wardrobe to find your favourite fox onesie. It's fluffy and warm. You can even pull the hood over your head if you want to ignore all of us."

Knowing her family and friends, Motts knew ignoring them wouldn't be an option. She headed into the bathroom anyway. A nice warm soak did sound brilliant.

"Are you covered?" Vina called through the door ten minutes later.

Motts shifted the suds to cover her body. "I'm fine."

Vina opened the door and set the onesie on the sink counter. "Prepare yourself. Your auntie and uncle, my parents, Marnie, and Inspector Ash have all arrived. Nish is trying to convince at least some of them to come back later."

"He'll be unsuccessful."

"Probably," Vina admitted. "Amma brought curry, your auntie brought what appears to be enough dumplings to feed all of Polperro, and Marnie brought Jaffa Cakes."

Waving Vina out of the bathroom, Motts decided she'd soaked and sulked enough. Nothing was going to change what had almost happened by the lighthouse. She didn't want to hide in the bathroom.

It made her feel as though she'd done something wrong. She might've been foolish to go out by the cliffs, but it hadn't been her fault. Noel was solely to blame for both Rhona's murder and attacking her.

Multiple times.

Motts dried off, pulled on her onesie, and dragged her brush through her hair. Cactus hopped up on the counter to observe. "Did I worry you?"

Meow.

"I apologise." She bent over to rub her nose against his. "How about a catnip biscuit?"

Lifting Cactus into her arms, Motts headed out to face the firing squad. Teo spotted her first; not a surprise when he stood taller than everyone in the room. She got the feeling he'd been watching for her.

"Hello, tiny Pineapple." Her uncle Tom surged forward to wrap his arms around her. He eased off when Cactus complained with a plaintive meow. "Are you alright, then?"

"I'm getting there, Uncle Tomato." Motts went from one hug to another. She finally made it into the kitchen and fished through the treat cupboard for one of Cactus's favourite biscuits. He ran off to hide behind the sofa to eat in peace. "Fine. Abandon me to face the interrogation alone."

When Motts turned towards everyone, the questions practically smacked her in the face. Everyone spoke over each other at varying volumes. She covered her ears with her hands and closed her eyes.

One. Two. Three. Four. Five. If I count to a hundred, will they all disappear?

Motts opened her eyes at the sound of movement to find the majority of those gathered were stepping out into the garden. She found herself alone with Teo, her uncle Tom, and Nish—the calmest of the bunch. "I never realised counting to ten was so powerful."

Nish winked at her. "They'll sort themselves out. Why don't you grab the Jaffa Cakes and a mug of hot chocolate? I heated the kettle for you."

Hot chocolate and biscuits in hand, Motts ensconced herself on her favourite section of the sofa. She draped a blanket over her legs. Cactus had finished his treat and leapt up to join her.

Her uncle Tom sat beside her while Nish and Teo sat on the armchairs across from the sofa. "Do you want to tell us what happened?"

Not really.

Ignoring her best friend and her uncle, Motts focused on Teo. She didn't understand why his presence comforted her, but it did. The three men listened while she talked through receiving the text from Danny to confronting Noel by the lighthouse.

They didn't seem at all comforted by how much she'd struggled to decide whether to go or not. She was grateful they didn't interrupt her tale. Teo had gotten out his little notebook to jot down notes when she shared what Noel had confessed.

"Is it safe to come in?" Vina poked her head into the cottage. "It's starting to rain again. I don't fancy all of us getting a chill."

"Come on. We can nosh on the mountain of food." Motts waved them inside. She'd shared all she intended to about her ill-advised adventure. "No more questions."

"But—"

Teo stood up, causing Vina to pause. "She's talked enough about the incident for one day. Leave her alone."

Motts smiled gratefully at him, and he winked in return. "Are you leaving?"

Teo nodded. He came around the room and bent down to kiss the top of her head. "I've a suspect to interrogate. You enjoy your curry and cakes."

"Teo?" She glanced up to meet his gaze. "Thank you."

CHAPTER TWENTY-FIVE

Over a month had passed since Motts's dramatic encounter by the lighthouse. All of her aches and pains had faded away within the first week. Her only lingering reminder was the occasional nightmare.

The bad dreams haunted her sleep at least twice a week. She had initially tried to stay up all night to avoid them. When that didn't work, she'd taken to calling Teo, who kindly talked through her nightmares with her until she managed to drift off peacefully.

Motts usually hated talking on the phone for any length of time. Teo didn't cause the same level of anxiety for some reason. She had the brief spike of fear when dialling his number, then it faded away after he answered.

After two weeks, Motts had begun to feel comfortable outside of the cottage once more. She got back into the habit of walking the path to fight her fears. Her daily forays into the village helped.

Over the first few days, it felt like every villager had popped by to check on her. Marnie had explained they'd taken Noel's behaviour as a personal affront and wanted to ensure Motts received a proper welcome. She didn't know how to deal with them or the copious amounts of food they brought.

But now, five weeks after the drama on the cliff, Motts had begun to settle down completely. She didn't jump at shadows. Any anxiety now likely had more to do with an impending visit from her parents, which would definitely involve an argument about her moving back home.

She wouldn't.

Despite everything, Motts had already fallen in love with life in the village. She'd created a new routine for herself. The garden had begun to flourish in the late spring sun.

She was happy.

Today she had a long day in the garden planned. Some of her herbs needed tending, and weeds always needed pulling. Teo had promised to stop by for a visit, since he had the entire weekend off.

"Knock, knock."

Motts sat back on her heels. She'd been pulling weeds from one of her plots of herbs. "I can see you over the gate. And I know you can reach the latch with your unnaturally long arms."

"I'd look rather strange if I had T-rex limbs." Teo demonstrated by pulling his arms up, causing her to laugh. He reached over the gate to unhook the latch and let himself into the garden. "My mother sends her love in the form of štrukli—it's like a cream cheese strudel of sorts."

Motts immediately stood up, yanking her gloves off and using them to brush the dirt away from her jeans. "You had me at cream cheese."

"Did I?"

She frowned at him, trying to decipher his tone of voice. "Question?"

"Flirting, not an actual question." He lifted the covered dish in his hands. "Have you worked up an appetite? I have."

"Doing what? Driving."

"It's a tough job." Teo smiled. She always felt a strange flutter in her stomach when he grinned. "I have news for you."

Motts went from the enjoyable flutter to a sinking sensation in her stomach. "Oh?"

"Not bad." He shifted the dish to one hand and

wrapped his arm around her shoulders. "The prosecutor wanted me to give you the latest update."

Deciding tea was needed, Motts led Teo into the cottage. Cactus immediately sauntered up to greet the detective inspector. He'd fallen in love with the man; not surprising when he brought treats for both of her pets on a frequent basis.

"Don't." Motts stopped Teo from speaking before he'd even opened his mouth. She washed her hands before filling the kettle and switching it on. "Tea, coffee, or cocoa?"

"Coffee."

Motts had already reached for her jar of instant coffee. She'd gotten it specifically for Teo, since he preferred it to tea. "How did I know?"

When they'd finally settled at the kitchen table with drinks and a slice of the not-quite strudel, Motts stirred her cocoa nervously. Teo sipped his coffee and waited. She appreciated his not pushing her into a conversation she didn't want to have.

Motts knew putting off the inevitable wouldn't help in the long run. "Go on, then."

"Are you sure?" Teo stretched his arm across the table and wrapped his hand around hers. "It can wait."

"Will I read about it in the paper?"

"Definitely. And I have no doubt village gossip

will be sharing the news." He squeezed her hand gently, then leaned back into his chair. "Noel has decided to plead guilty. His defence counsel made him understand forcing this to trial wouldn't gain him anything."

"So, I don't have to go to court." Motts had grown increasingly anxious the longer the case had gone on. Rhona deserved the justice that Jenny never received. "I would, but I wasn't looking forward to it. Vina said I had a good argument for Cactus being my emotional support animal."

Teo failed at trying to hide his smile behind his coffee mug. "I'm not laughing at you, I promise. I'm just imagining the crown court's reaction to a naked cat on the stand."

"He's not naked," Motts insisted. She wrapped her hands around her mug. "Mostly. So, what happens now?"

"He'll be sentenced. You don't have to worry about dealing with Noel ever again." Teo saluted her with his mug. "Now, with that out of the way, what are your plans for the day?"

"Weeding?" She hadn't finished with her garden chores.

"Gardening it is."

They hadn't done a ton of traditional dates. Teo

had taken her distaste for going to restaurants, the movies, or any crowded public place in stride. They'd gotten takeout a lot and gone for walks and bike rides all around southern Cornwall.

Their families had met. Her uncle Tom and auntie Lily had invited Teo and his parents for dinner. River had spent most of the meal teasing her endlessly until she accidently on purpose knocked her pot de crème into his lap, much to everyone's amusement.

They intended to have another meal when her parents arrived—at her uncle and auntie's place. Her cottage was simply too small. Motts had no idea how her mum and dad would handle her new relationship; River and Nish had promised to be there for moral support.

A week and a half later, their offer was being put to the test. Her uncle Tom had a sick sense of humour. He'd placed her parents and Teo's on the same side of the table, while they were on the opposite with River and Nish.

"Eat. Eat." Her auntie Lily had grown tired of everyone sitting in an uneasy silence around the table. "I didn't poison anything."

Teo exchanged a glance with Motts. "Should I take it as a good sign that she's joking about poisoning us in front of me?"

Motts turned away to laugh along with Nish, who'd heard Teo's comment. "I'm not explaining why this is funny."

The tension in the room slowly dissipated as the meal progressed. Her dad and Teo's seemed to get along well. Her mum, on the other hand, kept frowning at Teo.

"This is what happens when you flee the nest." River leaned around Nish to whisper to her. "She'll calm down eventually."

"Did Auntie Lily?"

River crossed both of his fingers. "Any day now. It helps that Nish is far more responsible than I am."

"And Teo isn't?"

"My mum isn't nearly as protective as yours," her cousin pointed out helpfully. "Your dad seems impressed by him."

"Teo saved his little poppet. Of course her dad loves him." Nish shoved River back into his seat. "You're drawing attention to yourselves."

They were halfway through dessert when the other shoe finally dropped. Motts had been holding her breath in the hopes she'd escape without being embarrassed by her parents. She'd almost gotten to the end when everything went haywire.

"And you, young man, what are your intentions

with our Motts?" Her mum pointed her cheesecake-covered fork at Teo. "Does a detective inspector make enough to support someone? Is it safe?"

Motts felt the flush start at the base of her neck and creep up her face. "Mum!"

"I worry, dear."

She set her fork down on the plate and tried to compose herself. She'd practised a response to this sort of conversation for days in preparation. "I make enough money from my business to support myself. Teo and I have barely begun dating. We only had this dinner because you and dad insisted."

"Poppet." Her dad draped his arm across the back of her mum's chair. "She worries."

"That's not a good enough excuse. You keep saying she worries as though it erases the damage she's started to do to our relationship." Motts shot to her feet, and Teo caught her chair to keep it from falling to floor. "I love you, Mum. I do. You can't keep treating me like I'm a teenager. I'm in sodding perimenopause, for crying out loud."

"Pineapple."

Motts held her hand up to stop her mum from responding. "Enough, Mum. You make me feel as though I'm incapable of managing my life. I'm not. At all."

Once again, Motts found herself fleeing to the garden. She sat on the steps and reconsidered all her life choices. Teo came out and joined her, squashing himself beside her.

"Sorry for the awkwardness." She wasn't embarrassed for speaking her mind. She should've stood up for herself months ago. "They love me. I think they just expected me to be somewhat dependent on them forever. I'm sorry they bombarded you with so many questions."

"Don't be." Teo eased Motts into a hug. He bent his head to brush a kiss against the top of her head. "Life isn't all about a walk down the primrose path. I'm just glad mine led to you."

The End

THANKS

Dahlia Donovan wrote her first romance series after a crazy dream about shifters and damsels in distress. She prefers irreverent humour and unconventional characters. An autistic and occasional hermit, her life wouldn't be complete without her husband and her massive collection of books and video games.

Join Dahlia's newsletter:
http://eepurl.com/QonoX
Join her Patreon:
www.patreon.com/dahliadonovan

Dahlia would love to hear from you directly, too. Please feel free to email her at dahlia@dahliadonovan.com or check out her website dahliadonovan.com for updates.

ACKNOWLEDGMENTS

A massive thank you to my brilliant betas who take my first draft and help me turn it into something legible. To Becky and Olivia, who always have faith in me. To all the fantastic people at Tangled Tree. And also to my beloved hubby, who keeps me from losing my mind while I'm stressing over word counts.

And, lastly, thank you, readers, for following me on my writing journey. I hope you enjoyed *Poisoned Primrose*. Motts is a character very close to my heart, and I hope you loved her as much as I do.

ABOUT THE PUBLISHER

As Hot Tree Publishing's first imprint branch, Tangled Tree Publishing aims to bring darker, twisted, more tangled reads to its readers. Established in 2015, they have seen rousing success as a rising publishing house in the industry motivated by their enthusiasm and keen eye for talent. Driving them is their passion for the written word of all genres, but with Tangled Tree Publishing, they're embarking on a whole new adventure with words of mystery, suspense, crime, and thrillers.

Join the growing Hot Tree Group family of authors, promoters, editors, and readers. Become a part of not just a company but an actual family by submitting your manuscript to Tangled Tree Publishing.

Know that they will put your interests and book first, and that your voice and brand will always be at the forefront of everything they do.

For more details, head to www.tangledtreepublishing.com.

CPSIA information can be obtained
at www.ICGtesting.com
Printed in the USA
BVHW031816260720
584699BV00001B/2